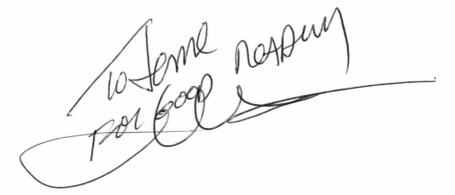

Remme's Ride
For The Gold

Thorn Bacon

BookPartners, Inc.
Wilsonville, Oregon

Illustrations by Richard Ferguson
Portland, Oregon

BookPartners, Inc.
P.O. Box 922
Wilsonville,Oregon 97070

Dedication

This is for Ursula, always.

Author's Note

The drama and excitement of men on horseback racing through the pages of history have made a deep imprint on readers. No story of men in the West is more remarkable than that of Louis Remme who changed horses more than twenty times in a wild 700-mile race with a steamboat to rescue a fortune in gold.

Remme's Ride For The Gold is based on the actual events surrounding the legendary horseback ride of Louis Remme in February 1855 from Sacramento, California to Portland, Oregon. While short versions of his story have appeared in *American Heritage Magazine* and the *Oregon Business Review*, the original account of Remme's ride was published in the *Sunday Oregonian* February 12, 1882.

The version of Remme's ride presented in this book is based on the published facts about his journey. The author has been careful to adhere to a faithful description of the route Remme took, the people who helped him along the way and the obstacles he had to overcome in the dead of winter to reach Portland, Oregon in six days.

It was a brisk February day in San Francisco when Louis Remme sat down to breakfast in his hotel dining room. A slender, wiry man of medium height, Remme was dressed for the city in a gray wool suit, red string tie and polished black boots. He felt elegant seated at a table covered with starched white linen with a matching napkin stuffed in a polished oyster shell ring. A tall silvered pot of coffee rested next to his cup of bone china and for his reading pleasure a copy of the *California Chronicle* thoughtfully had been placed neatly folded on the table.

Remme was amused at himself. He had never

treated himself to the luxury of a grand hotel like the St. Francis which was host to the rich and famous of San Francisco. The fancy room he had rented was priced at $28 a day, a lot of money for a French-Canadian cattle trader who only a week earlier had completed a long, muddy cattle drive down the Sacramento valley from northern California. The rooms he was used to sleeping in cost $1 per night and the papered walls breathed in and out when the wind was blowing. But he was celebrating the sale of the last of his cattle herd and had found himself with $12,500 in gold, more money than he had ever possessed at one time in his life. On a whim, after he deposited his gold at the Sacramento branch of Adams Express Company, he had taken the steamer to San Francisco with $1,000 in his pocket. He was going to enjoy himself for a few days visiting the opera, the museums, San Francisco's famous waterfront restaurants and he intended to risk a few dollars in the gambling houses which had a reputation for gaiety and entertainment.

When he checked into the St. Francis, looking prosperous in his dark wool suit, he seemed at home, unintimidated by the plush surroundings and thick Persian rugs. The clerk at the registration desk sized up Remme as a man who was rising in the world and offered him a room with a grand brass bed and velvet drapes. He accepted gracefully.

As he finished his breakfast eggs on his first day in the hotel, and sipped his second cup of coffee, Remme thought about how San Francisco had changed in the seven years since a gold nugget had been found in Sutter's Mill starting the Forty-Niner gold rush. From a sleepy town slumbering on a lovely bay, San Francisco had been transformed into a tent city by thousands of miners who rushed to answer the call of gold. In a few years it had grown into a bustling city with tall buildings, magnificent homes and a population of 250,000 people. Remme had occupied the years of San Francisco's gold rush growth differently than most of the men who traveled to California. While San Francisco was prospering and changing, he had learned cattle trading the hard way. Starting with nothing when he left Quebec in French-speaking Canada almost a decade earlier, he had drifted south and west into California territory. He had learned about cattle and horses in a dozen different jobs, working as a mule skinner's helper, a cattle drover's apprentice, a wild horse tamer. He had driven wagons, toiled in the gold mines and found that not to his liking, and had farmed for one season. He had repaired wagon wheels, learned to shape steel shoes for horses in a smithy's fire and discovered that he liked to work leather for relaxation. He found his niche when he started locating "brush hoppers," domesticated cattle that strayed from herds and went wild. It was cruel, brutal, dangerous work driving stubborn steers used to their freedom—animals that could rip a man with their horns for no reason other than their contrary natures.

Little by little, Remme became known in the Oregon and northern California frontier as a shrewd trader, trapping and fattening wild cattle, building small herds he drove to pioneer towns where settlers needed animals for breeding at reasonable prices. He was especially appealing to lonely settlers who were starved for conversation and excitement in their lives. He was a romantic, cheerful figure when he showed up dressed in leather and wool with jingling spurs, mounted on a lean, fast horse, a man who could always be counted on to carry a message to the next farm or to mail a letter with a favorite recipe in a town large enough to have a stage coach. He was referred to as "that crazy Frenchman" not only because he sang songs with lilting, strange words to himself, ones he had learned as a child in Quebec, but because he was admired for his free, daring life. He had a dark complexion, large brown eyes, a quick smile and long black hair that grew to shoulder length when he was away months at a time trading for cows and building a herd.

As Remme spread butter on a hot biscuit, he realized how fortunate he was to be sitting in a fancy hotel cheerfully contemplating his future. For the first time in all the years he had been trading cattle, he had enough money in the bank to put the down payment on a cherished dream. His dream was a cattle ranch flowing with cool water and sweet grass on which he could graze and fatten cows for market. San Francisco paid handsomely for beef and its growing population couldn't seem to get enough. It was Remme's idea to drive cattle from collection points in the Sacramento and San Juaquin Valleys to San Francisco in stages. By herding cattle slowly, the animals could graze along the way, put on weight and arrive in the city fat and healthy. Of course, stockmen drove herds of cattle into the holding pens in the city every day. But most of the cows arrived in poor condition, thirsty, exhausted and thinner than when they started on the trail. Remme's idea was to reverse the process.

By controlling the pace of the cattle drive, the cows would be less nervous, lose less fat and bring a much higher price when they arrived at the stockyards. He was surprised that no one else had thought of his plan. It just made sense. Buyers would pay more for plump cattle than skinny critters with trail-hardened muscles. Actually, he knew why most cattlemen in northern California didn't bother to put pounds on the cattle they raised. There was such a high demand by gold-rush miners for beef that a butcher could sell whang leather and call it steak.

But times were changing. After all, it was 1855! San Francisco was growing up and so were the tastes of its citizens. There were a dozen theaters in the city by the bay. Men and women who had endured the hardships of the gold rush years wanted more comfort and the good things of life. His own hotel, the St. Francis—the first to put sheets on the beds instead of the customary scratchy blankets which used to irritate the guests—sponsored fancy dress balls and appearances at social gatherings of famous actors and singers. Why, he had learned that the American Thrush, Eliza Biscaccianti had dared to brave wild and boisterous San Francisco when other singers such as Jenny Lind and Catherine

Hayes had declined. Was it any wonder that natives of San Francisco who had endured the the gold-rush diet of beans and bacon, wanted more comfort and better food? Tender steaks and roasts which he would soon provide from the pampered cattle he drove to town would be part of the new future.

He already had his eye on a cattle ranch of 3,000 acres near Grass Valley, north of Sacramento. The gold he had on deposit in the Adams Express Bank would make the purchase of the land and buildings possible. Caught up in his pleasant view of himself prospering on his Grass Valley ranch, Remme was spooning sugar into his third cup of coffee when he overheard a snatch of conversation from a neighboring table. The statement that caught his attention was spoken by a man to his breakfast companion.

"I heard the steamer *Oregon* arrived yesterday with some bad news. Page, Bacon and Company of St. Louis has gone broke. The story is that it had to suspend business because of bad loans to the Ohio and Mississippi Railroad. That means our own Page, Bacon Bank here is in big trouble since it is a branch. People are in a panic here, taking their money out of the bank. A small run started here this morning. My question is will the bank have enough gold to pay everybody? I'm glad I don't have my money in the bank."

Remme found the man's news only slightly disquieting. He was certain his own gold resting securely in the vault of Adams Express Company Bank in Sacramento was absolutely safe, but it was unsettling to hear that one of the oldest banks in the west had gone broke. The failure of the old, reliable St. Louis bank would send shivers through depositors in the San Francisco branch. The question raised was could the local bank, lacking the backing and gold reserves of the parent bank, survive the sudden rush of depositors for their money? The shrewd cattle trader knew that the fate of Page, Bacon and Company in San Francisco would depend on how panicky its customers became. If the bank could keep paying until worried folks regained their confidence and stopped withdrawing their gold, then everything would be alright.

Concerned more than he wanted to admit, Remme decided to discover if the man at the next table had any more details to impart to his companion. He inclined his head to listen, pretending to read his newspaper.

"I don't know if the panic is bad enough to spread to other banks, but I think I am going to see my bank as soon as we're finished here. Better to be safe than sorry. I did hear that Page, Bacon has a connection to Adams Express Bank. I wonder if it's true?"

The reference to Adams Express Company struck Louis Remme like a splash of cold water in his face. He dropped his napkin, rose to his feet and stepped to the neighboring table.

"Excuse me, gentlemen," he said, his eyes resting on the larger of the two seated men. "I couldn't help but overhear your conversation, and your statement, sir, that Adams Express Bank may be linked to Page, Bacon. I have money in Adams. May I ask how reliable your information is?"

Both men were gracious about Remme's intrusion and the one who had been talking said, "I don't know how reliable it is, but I think Adams Express is on shaky ground" The man frowned, then looked sympathetically at Remme and added, "If I were you I guess I'd try to get my money out. Better to be safe than sorry."

Remme apologized to the men for his interruption, turned to his table where he dropped a few coins next to his breakfast plate for the waiter and walked into the hotel lobby. A dozen questions popped into his mind as he considered what his next move should be and he couldn't dismiss the sinking feeling in his stomach. Was it possible that a bank's failure half a continent away could have an echo in San Francisco? Could his personal fortune be in jeopardy? How bad was the panic? If it spread to other banks in San Francisco, the chances of it influencing his own bank in Sacramento, only sixty miles away, were probably predictable. The aspect of the bank run that worried him most was the statement that had electrified him a minute ago—a rumor that Adams Express was linked to the troubled Page, Bacon bank. If that rumor grew, if Adams Express depositors got wind of what he had heard, he knew they would start clamoring wildly for their savings. Remme had to admit to himself that his own unfounded suspicions about Adams Express were growing by leaps and bounds.

A man who acted quickly when his mind was made up, Remme decided to wait no longer. He would cut his vacation short and catch the next boat upriver to Sacramento. Even as he made up his mind, he prayed to himself that he would not be too late. He realized as he paid the bill for his room and checked out of his hotel that he was acting hastily. He had absolutely no information beyond a single overheard conversation that his bank might be the target of a run simply by association with Page,

Bacon and Company. As he tipped the hotel doorman, asking him to whistle for a horse and carriage,
he was determined to put a brake on his imagination. After all, the boat to Sacramento did not leave
San Francisco until late afternoon. He had several
hours to kill. Also a pair of boots he had ordered
from a reliable boot maker on Sutter Street would
not be ready before 2:00 p.m. It was only 11:00 a.m.

When Remme climbed into the carriage that
responded to the call of the doorman, he told the
cheerful driver to take him to the city's main square,
Portsmouth Plaza. Many of the San Francisco's
banking institutions were located in the plaza.
Remme had some time to kill before the steamer
left in the afternoon for Sacramento. He was going
to visit the offices of Adams Express Company
Bank located in the plaza. He didn't know what he
was going to say to the people at the bank, but he
was certain he would have to be cautious and crafty
if he was going to learn anything valuable about
the soundness of the bank. While the certificate he
owned proving he had $12,500 in gold on deposit in
the Sacramento branch of Adams Express was resting in the safe at his boarding house in Sacramento,
and could not be cashed unless he presented it in
person to a teller or agent, Remme's idea was to

gather any information which could help him to make a decision about withdrawing his gold. He doubted that the San Francisco officials of Adams Express were going to admit to him that their bank was in trouble, even if it was. But he hadn't learned over the years to trade shrewdly for cattle without discovering how to judge the motives of men, often by what they didn't say.

It had been four years since Remme had visited Portsmouth Plaza and he didn't recognize it when he stepped down from his carriage and paid the driver. He was amazed at what he saw. Hundreds of people—men in frock coats and top hats, workmen in aprons, women in long skirts, sailors in blue jackets and brass buttons, flower sellers with baskets of asters, sweet peas and chrysanthemums oblivious to the raw February weather, walked and mingled and exchanged comments and words along the wooden plank sidewalks.

The plaza was ringed with the offices of attorneys, doctors, dentists, banks, and brokerages. The old adobe city hall occupied the north edge of the square. The city's courthouse, customhouse and surveying offices rested not far from the Parker House, Denison's Exchange and the Empire Hotel that boasted they were fireproof. Not to be missed were several saloons, a laundry, a public school-house and a gristmill.

Remme was overwhelmed by the changes. He remembered the square as a wild area of shanties and tents and cow pens and grassy mounds where animals grazed. Now, it was a bustling modern plaza with a flag to identify its public character and an atmosphere of busy commerce and enthusiasm.

As he got directions to the building in which Adams Express Company was housed, Remme realized it had been natural for companies which originally had been organized to deliver mail to thousands of California miners to merge with financial institutions that kept gold for customers. Like Adams Express Company, the more famous Wells Fargo had started in business just three years earlier in 1852 to transport mail. It was transformed into a banking company, spurred by the demands of miners for a safe place to deposit their gold. The flow of wealth from the incredible gold rush caused many express and banking companies to join together and they had grown tremendously prosperous. Could an established firm like Adams be in trouble? Remme wondered as he walked up the stairs of the bank. Was it hiding something rotten that the public didn't know about?

The idea that Adams Express Company may have failed in its trust to its customers and might be concealing the facts about its rumored association with the floundering Page, Bacon and Company gave Remme a strengthened sense of resolve when he entered the offices of the bank. On the surface, everything appeared normal. Several customers stood in front of tellers cages transacting business. Remme saw stacks of gold coins changing hands and there was a pleasant chink of metal, the rustle of currency and the air of privacy typical of financial institutions. No one appeared hurried, or anxious. His eyes finally came to a stop on a stern man with heavy sideburns seated at a desk behind a wooden banister. With his slight paunch, dark gray suit, blue foulard tie, he looked like a person whose job was important.

Deciding on a story to cover the real reason for his presence in the bank, Remme removed his wide-brimmed hat, stepped up to the railing and said courteously to the seated bank official, "I am a depositor in the Sacramento branch of Adams. I am in San Francisco on a holiday and I need to know about shipping some gold dust to Sonora. Can you help me?"

The sun came out on the banker's face as he

smiled at Remme and invited him to push through
the wooden gate in the railing and take a chair
beside the desk. When Remme told the man whose
name was Harold Forbes that he was staying at the
St. Francis, the banker's attitude became respect-
ful. It was obvious to him that Remme was a man of
substance, a person whose bank patronage was
valuable. After exchanging pleasantries with his
visitor and discovering that Remme was a cattle
trader, Forbes poised a pencil in his hand above a
small white pad on his desk and said, " You spoke
about shipping dust to Sonora, how much did you
have in mind, Mr. Remme? You know we charge
one half of one percent as our fee for transporting
gold."

Remme put a frown on his forehead, pretending
to be suddenly disturbed and thoughtful. He shifted
in his chair and hesitated as if he were reluctant to
say what was on his mind. Finally, he said, lowering
his voice, "The sum I have in mind is quite large.
I…"

"And you're concerned about its safety? Is that
it, Mr. Remme?"

"Exactly," Remme whispered with a relieved
sigh and looked worriedly into the eyes of the
banker.

Smiling largely, Forbes leaned across his desk and said reassuringly, "Banish your doubts, my friend. Our shipments are carefully protected. After all, Adams Express Bank has a reputation for prudence and caution."

"Then the rumor about Adams being associated in the failure of Page, Bacon and Company is false?"

Forbes tried to cover up the stab of panic in his eyes from Remme's surprise question, but it was too late. His sudden cautious expression gave him away. He cleared his throat and said hurriedly, "I don't know what you mean." But Remme was already on his feet. He knew now that his whole future was in peril. He had to get to Sacramento as soon as possible and recover his gold. And he knew as he left the bank that Forbes, furious for being tricked, would never have told him whether or not Adams Express was on the verge of closing. And he was absolutely certain the banker would not have told him if fast riders had already been dispatched to the dozen or so branches of Adams Express in northern California with secret instructions to close down if the rumor grew and depositors started clamoring for their gold.

2

It was 6:00 P.M. Thursday, February 22nd, when Remme hurried down the gangplank of the paddle wheel steamer *Rosebud* and slogged rapidly through the trampled, clinging mud until he reached the center of Sacramento Town, his boots heavy with clumps of brown clay. He passed the City Hotel, formerly John Sutter's old grist mill, which had been transformed into a fancy palace where miners could eat, drink, gamble and sometimes sleep. The hotel was ablaze with lights and noisy with music and raised voices as Remme trudged by, then turned a street and paused on the wooden porch of his boarding house. A flat iron boot scraper with a sharp edge hung from a string tied to a nail imbedded in a board next to the doorsill. As he propped first one foot then the other on a wooden stump sticking out of the ground under the nail and scraped mud in thick layers from his boots, Remme thought about how his San Francisco vacation had ended with his discovery of treachery at his bank.

After leaving Forbes behind his railing at the express company office, and stopping off to pay for his new boots, then hiring an open carriage to take him to the waterfront, Remme bought a late lunch and waited three hours for the steamer to start loading passengers for Sacramento. He was impatient to get upstream and realized there was nothing he could do until the next day when first thing, he would take his certificate of deposit to the Sacramento offices of Adams Express Company at 46 Second Street.

His boots clean, Remme opened the door and climbed the front stairs of Miller's Boardinghouse to the second floor. He hoped he would not encounter anybody; he was in no mood for idle talk. He unlocked the door to his room and dropped his leather suitcase and the package containing his new boots on his bed. Once in the familiar surroundings of his own room and his few valued personal possessions he felt better. On the wall there was a colorful Mexican shawl that once belonged to a Santa Fe beauty who cared for him. On a chest of drawers was a framed photo of his mother and himself. He was in a long dress and stood at her knee. He had been five years old. On the lamp-stand next to his bed rested a pistol with a dark walnut handle. It had been given to him by John Charles Fremont before he became California's first U.S. senator.

Remme decided to put the whole Adams Express Bank business out of his mind. There was nothing he could do until the morning and worry never accomplished anything. He fell into a restless sleep an hour after eating supper and he dreamed of swimming in a clear stream near the farm in Quebec where he grew up as a boy. He cast off his clothes in his dream and he felt the current of the river soothing and lifting his bare, lean body and he enjoyed the cool ooze of the mud between his toes. Then he heard his dog barking excitedly, her sharp voice overriding his splashing and the smooth hissing and agreeable rumble of the river. He looked up then, scanning the river bank. Through the moving curtain of spray and foam he saw his dog was circling a figure in agitation. It was a man and he was growing bigger and bigger as he drew closer to the river bank.

Remme was frightened as the man's form filled out, became taller and wavered like a person formed out of fog, a ghost in a story, and he huddled in the stream, growing cold as he stood with his shoulders out of the water. Then he recognized the long sideburns on the man's pale cheeks, the deep scowl in his face, the slight paunch of his stomach, the dark gray suit and the blue foulard tie. It was the banker, Forbes, who stood holding Remme's clothes and stared at him angry-eyed and frighteningly unfamiliar.

Remme felt himself pushing through the water toward the bank, unable to stop his legs from pulling him forward. He started up the slippery bank, naked and ashamed, to meet Forbes who had lifted a heavy stick in his right hand over his head and was bringing it down toward Remme's head with a whizzing, hissing sound. Remme woke up then, saving himself from the banker's blow. He breathed deeply for a few moments, then stared out of the window of his room at the bright moon hanging serenely in the blue. The rain had stopped, the clouds had disappeared and a cluster of stars like icy brilliant diamonds pierced the sky. It was near dawn. He felt the warmth of his blankets and slipped into a light doze and then he was wandering over the wooded hills behind his old home in Quebec.

Even though Remme arrived at the Second Street office building of Adams Express fully thirty minutes before the normal opening hour of 9:00 A.M. on Friday, his heart sank. The worst of his fears had come true. At least twenty grumbling, loud-talking men were assembled in front of the wooden doors bristling with anger as they patiently waited for clerks inside the bank to raise the window shades and turn the locks. The cat was out of the bag. The San Francisco rumor describing Adams Express's involvement with the bankrupt Page, Bacon and Company had traveled 60 miles overnight. The question was whether or not the express company was going to honor drafts or suspend payments.

Remme had obtained his certificate of deposit from the boardinghouse safe in his landlord's small office and now it rested securely in his pocket. But he doubted seriously whether he was going to be able to redeem its face value. As if in answer to his question on the dot of nine a slender, middle-aged man with thinning hair, wearing a black suit opened the front doors to the bank and pushed carefully through the crowd of men that was still growing and he stood on the steps of the bank.

"I have a notice to read," he said in a high voice. "When I have finished I will tack it to the outside of the door for anybody who wishes to examine it."

Fastening reading glasses on his nose and clearing his throat, he held the notice between his hands and read:

"The undersigned, resident partner in Sacramento of Adams Express Company of California, announces suspension of payment on this date, February 23, 1855, on all certificates of deposit, notes or acceptances, sight drafts or checks drawn upon the Adams Express Company..."

Howls of protest drowned the clerk's voice and several men in a rage started up the steps with the obvious intent to charge into the bank. Curiously, they stopped when the clerk raised his hand and he said calmly, "Violence will not help matters. I have a brief statement of the causes that led to this calamity."

He paused, looked gravely at the gathered men and said, "It is well known that the demand for gold for shipment has for months far exceeded the supply of gold dust from the mines. As a result gold coin has been withdrawn from circulation at a rate of about one million dollars per month. This has left scarcely enough for the most ordinary needs of business, and it has caused unusual pressure for gold. This pressure has resulted in today's announcement."

As if on cue just as the clerk completed his explanation, two burly men carrying shotguns and wearing badges on their coats stepped from behind the door of the bank and positioned themselves stiffly on each side of the clerk. It was clear they were on hand to protect the bank from anybody who decided to take matters into his own hands and force the bank to pay out what it owed.

It was Remme who stepped forward and asked the question that was on the mind of every man in the crowd, "Is the bank closed for good or is there a chance we can get our gold in a few days?"

The clerk looked down at Remme with a slight smirk on his face. "Sir," he said, "Adams Express Company is in liquidation. The receiver, Mr. Alfred Cohen, will decide on its future."

"In plain language the bank is broke! That's what you mean isn't it?" an angry man in the crowd shouted.

Another man yelled, "I hear Woods has disappeared? Is it true? How much of our money did he take with him?"

The clerk stepped back cautiously and the deputies looked sharply at the man in the crowd for any sign of sudden violence.

Remme turned away bitter with disappointment. The shock of his loss was so great that for a moment he could not accept what had happened to him. He looked around and saw on the faces of the men who were drifting away a mirror of his own anger and loss. He had less than a thousand dollars in the world. He was almost broke after six years of backbreaking work chasing and corralling obstinate steers. When he tricked the banker Forbes in San Francisco yesterday and learned Adams was in trouble, he had still hoped for the best, even though in his heart he had known his gold was probably lost. Now, everything he had worked for was gone. The ranch in Grass Valley was a foolish dream now, out of reach of a man who owned little more than a saddle, the clothes on his back, a few hundred dollars and some personal possessions. The idea that he was back where he started six years before was unsettling for the 34-year-old French Canadian whose confidence in himself to face any obstacle in nature with strength and nerve had never proved to be wrong. Now, because of the dishonesty of men in banks he did not even know, his whole future was wiped out.

As Remme started back to his boardinghouse, he could guess what was happening when other men and women in California towns that housed branches of Adams Express Company inquired about their gold: Locked doors and sheriff's deputies protecting the closed banks. He had considered and discarded the idea of finding a horse and making a wild dash to Adams branches in Marysville or Grass Valley and cash his draft there. But he knew the news of the failure would be ahead of him everywhere he tried to get relief. Had Remme but known it, just a few minutes earlier, the citizens of Sonora, California, learning the news of the bank collapse from a messenger who had ridden all night, had taken matters into their own hands. A mob in a hanging mood overpowered the sheriff and his deputies and broke into the Sonora office. The citizens confiscated the gold in the vaults and forced the express company clerks at gunpoint to count it out among its rightful owners.

Lower than he had ever been in his life, Remme trudged down the muddy street unable to plan what he should do next. His mind seemed frozen with his personal disaster. Then, on an impulse which he could never later explain, he bent over and picked up a square of paper he saw lying in the mud. It probably had been discarded by one of the men in the crowd at the bank. It was a handbill advertising the overland stage routes and the major towns in California where Adams Express Company had branch offices. It was dated February 16, 1855, a week exactly to the day before the bank had failed.

It took a moment for Remme to fully understand what he was reading, then he became excited. An idea was growing in his mind. His eyes widened as he read the information in the handbill and his heart started pounding. Could this piece of paper be his salvation? If what he read was true there was a chance, slim, preposterous, yes, even mad, but a chance, that he could recover his savings. Frowning deeply, he scanned the bold print carefully for a moment longer, then three lines of black print leaped out at him:

We send a semi-monthly express to Oregon by mail steamer.

Remme's thoughts raced: the mail steamer, of course! The Pacific Mail Steamship *Columbia* made a twice monthly trip to Portland, Oregon. And, Adams Express Company had an agent in

Portland who could not know about the San Francisco disaster until the *Columbia's* purser brought the news!

With a shaking hand, Remme examined the handbill again. There in smaller type he found these words:

This is to certify that Dr. Steinberger is the only authorized person in Portland, Oregon to receive packages of gold to be forwarded by us from San Francisco, and to honor checks, notes or acceptances, and sight drafts, drawn upon the Adams Express Company.

Even as he crumpled the handbill and thrust it in his pocket, Remme's legs were carrying him in a dead run toward his boarding house. And his brain was moving just as swiftly, calculating the odds for the success of an impossible scheme: Could he beat the *Columbia* to Portland by horseback overland? He would have to ride through trackless forests, deep snow, wild rivers and craggy mountains. If he could do it, he could turn disaster into triumph by exchanging the now worthless sight draft in his wallet for $12,500 in gold from Dr. Steinberger.

Almost in the same instant he conceived the idea of the ride, he discarded the thought of going down river to San Francisco and catching the steamer itself. Even if he could get to San Francisco in time to board the boat before it left for Oregon, he would be a passenger and the news of the failure of Adams Express would be riding along with him. Then, unless he was the first person off of the boat when it arrived in Portland, he would face the same disappointment he had experienced in Sacramento.

Because of Indian troubles between the Klamath and the Rogue Rivers in Oregon and also in the Pit River country, as well as the lack of passable roads, there was no stagecoach service between Sacramento and Portland and no telegraph. The Pacific Mail Steamship *Columbia* would be the first vessel to reach Portland carrying the news of the bank failure and clearly, unless Remme was willing to forget the gold he had worked so hard to accumulate, he would have to ride to Portland and beat the boat.

He knew it was 800 miles to Portland by water; six days for the *Columbia* to plod her way up the treacherous Pacific Coast to Astoria, Oregon, then down the Columbia River and into the Willamette River which passed the city of Portland. There she would dock. The reason it took so long for the *Columbia* to reach Portland was because of the several stops the steamship made on her trip north. The

Columbia picked up passengers and cargo first at Mendocino Mills, then at Humboldt Bay where Union soldiers were stationed. The next stops were at Trinidad, then Crescent City—the jumping-off point for the mining country of Northern California. The next stop for the paddle-wheel steamship in Oregon Territory was at the large military post at Gardner. Basically, the *Columbia* sailed in a straight line with a few side excursions, but the distance to Portland by horseback, as the crow flies, was just shy of 700 miles.

Only 700 miles! For that matter it may as well have been 7,000 miles! For a moment the wiry French Canadian's heart sank. Ahead of him lay some of the cruelest natural hazards in the American West. Some of the highest mountains in the continent raised their snowy heads in the Cascade Range. And they plunged into some of the deepest valleys with the fastest rivers, and the densest forests on earth. They climbed over rugged hills and pushed through valleys where the Coast Range tied to the Sierra Nevada. There were no well defined trails through the wilderness of Northern California and the Oregon Territory, only the pony forest paths of hostile indians and the few scattered white settlers. To make matters worse, within 200 miles he would encounter a killing obstacle: the deep drifts and ice that locked the higher elevations in a wintry grip. He could only pray that snowfall had been light on the upland reaches.

In his room at his boardinghouse, after he had stopped to buy supplies at a general merchandise store, Remme was slightly giddy at the boldness of his undertaking. If he had not spent years in the California-Oregon wilderness, he might not have been so aware of the dangers ahead of him. Dozens of brash, foolish men—prospectors, trappers, hunters—disappeared every year because they challenged the wilderness without experience or respect for its harshness. They were smashed to death in a dozen violent ways. Not only was Remme going to pit himself against the mountains and the raw elements in the dead of winter when the hazards were multiplied, but he was going to have to push himself far beyond ordinary endurance to have a chance to win his solitary race. The fact that he would have to ride at a breakneck pace also meant increasing the risk of accidents or the single mistake that could take his life.

Among the purchases Remme had made at the store was a one pound sack of coffee beans. On long night vigils in the past he had chewed on the bitter beans, strong with caffeine, to keep awake. Since he had to travel light, but knew body warmth was vital, he packed a spare pair of longjohns, the red woolen underwear that would keep much of his body heat from escaping. There were three pounds of beef jerky to chew on in the saddle, a spare shirt, two dozen hard biscuits, six cans of beans, three jars of peaches, four candles, two wooden clothes-pins, matches and a new flint with punk, two boxes of bullets for his rifle, three pairs of heavy long woolen stockings, earmuffs, wooden snowshoes and a long heavy woolen scarf.

With his saddle bags, his sheepskin coat, a heavy wool blanket tied in a roll and two canteens to add to his own body weight of 155 pounds, Remme would be asking the horses he rode to carry more than 200 pounds. The load was still lighter than the average a strong horse was used to bearing, but, every pound Remme gained in reduced load meant extra miles for mounts that would carry him.

Into a thin leather pouch, Remme carefully placed his certificate of deposit. Then he inserted the leather pouch into an oilskin envelope which he tied securely with string. He thrust the oilskin envelope into a space between his shirt and under-shirt.

3

It was 11 o'clock Friday morning, February 23, the day that many Californians later were to call Black Friday because of bank failures in San Francisco, that Remme caught a small paddle wheel steamer north from Sacramento to Knight's Landing. As he road north on the river, watching waves curl under the bow of the little steamer, Remme learned from a passenger returning from San Francisco that the odds against him had been increased. The *Columbia* had weighed anchor even while Remme thought up his impossible idea. There was no time to lose. He dared not even stop to think that his cause was hopeless, and that even supposing he could find the horses to make the grueling trip ahead of him—and he would need at least twenty hardy ponies capable of bearing him long distances at a steady run—how was he going to hold up to almost a week of continuous days and nights in the saddle without sleep?

When Remme carried his saddle, saddle bags packed with his provisions, and his bedroll off of the steamer, Lydia, at Knight's Landing, he looked almost like a different man. Gone was his dark suit, string tie and the shiny black boots. Instead, he wore the new rough, cowhide boots he bought in San Francisco. They covered his legs up to his knees. His buckskin pants, wrapped tightly around his legs, were thrust into the top of his boots. His long sheepskin coat worn open now, reached almost to his knees. Around his waist, he wore a wide belt to which was attached a sheath for a long sharp knife with an elkhorn handle. Another belt, riding lower on his hips, supported a dark brown leather holster with a row of cartridges. The belt held the black pistol given to Remme by John Charles Fremont. It was loaded and ready to fire.

With his saddle thrown over his shoulder, his heavy flat-brimmed felt hat pulled snugly down over his forehead, Remme could never be taken for the smiling dandy who had sipped coffee in the dining room of the St. Francis Hotel. Even his expression was changed. His piercing brown eyes in his lean face looked fierce beneath his heavy black brows and his jaw was set in a determined thrust as he strode down the gangplank of the Lydia and walked briskly toward the livery stable where he purchased a solid roan horse, a mare, for $80 and threw his saddle and bedroll on her back. He checked to make certain his range rifle was resting securely in its leather sling, mounted his new horse and clattered out onto the trail north.

Remme soon discovered the roan needed little urging to stretch her legs to their maximum stride and he let the animal have her head until she began to falter and show signs of fatigue as they neared Grand Isle several hours later.

Remme had carefully planned ahead of time how to exchange winded horses with friends without disturbing them. He didn't want to have to take the time to explain his mission to men with whom he traded horses until he absolutely had to. To begin with they might think he was crazy to be racing overland against a steamship. Then, when they decided he was actually trying to restore his life savings in an impossible race, they would probably want to know more about the bank failures and he would have to waste precious minutes to explain. Also, when some of them learned that he was going to push the horses he borrowed, or bought to the limits of their endurance, they might try to pawn off on him second rate animals, fearing he would ruin good ponies by riding them too hard.

Remme knew that as long as he rode within two hundred miles of Sacramento, his name would be known and trusted by anyone he was likely to borrow a horse from. He hit upon the idea of leaving a hand written note pinned to the mane of each horse he had to leave behind. The wooden clothespins he packed in his belongings were for this purpose.

The first note he wrote was addressed to an old friend of his, Judge Diefendorf at Grand Island. It read:

"Judge: I borrowed your sorrel. In an awful hurry chasing a horse thief. I am leaving the roan. She's a sound animal and you've got the best of the bargain. I'll see you in about a month. Yours, Louis Remme."

Remme had to chuckle to himself as he tightened the cinch of his saddle on the big sorrel and leaped into the familiar leather seat. His idea of blaming a nonexistent horse thief for his hurry was a good touch. There was no crime in the west considered to be worse than stealing a horse. Murderers got lighter sentences in a miner's court than a horse thief who often was hanged on the spot. Remme's friends would understand in an instant the urgency of a chase after a horse thief. When they found a strange horse with his note, they would wish him luck and God-speed. Of course the note acknowledging the exchange of horses was very important. That's why it had to be secured on the horse in a fashion that guaranteed it would be found and not flicked off. The clothes pins would do the trick, Remme decided, even if rain wetted the paper. He smiled as he looked at the note paper pinned high on the roan's mane where it grew between her ears. It was a safe place. The horse couldn't reach it to dislodge it, and it looked pretty, almost like a decorative bow.

The next thirty miles took Remme past Marysville and into Brown's Valley. He pulled Judge Diefendorf's winded sorrel pony to a halt in a pasture where several mares were grazing. The animal he was riding was tired and breathing heavily as he walked it slowly toward the clustered horses whose ears started twitching as they raised their heads and stared at the intruder. Remme's eyes were on a gray, a sleek, long- legged mare with a blaze on her forehead. Carefully, he shook out his lariat and let the loop dangle harmlessly next to his right boot.

When he kneed the sorrel as close to the mares as he dared to without spooking them, Remme suddenly swung his lariat in a large flowing circle that dropped over the head of the gray fifteen feet away, even as the mares bolted and ran. Quickly, Remme wrapped the free end of his rope around the pommel of his saddle to keep it from being jerked out of his hand as the gray lunged against the loop. Dropping to the ground, he ran to the gray and pulled her head down. She quieted as he murmured to her and smoothed her neck with one hand.

Ten minutes later, Remme, aboard the tall, slender gray, clattered swiftly out of the pasture, headed north. He smiled to himself as he thought about the owner and what she would say to herself about Remme when she found the strange sorrel horse with the note clothes-pinned to her mane.

Remme had known the gray's owner, Lola Montez, for two years ever since she moved to a plain small cottage in Grass Valley where she lived by herself with a brown bear on a chain, dogs, parrots, cats and a goat. He had discovered that Lola, a blond-haired, rosy-cheeked, black-eyed beauty, had been the favorite of European kings and bore the title Countess of Landsfeldt. She had appeared in famous California theaters as the Spider Woman. She had amazed crowds with her wild dance in which spiders made from cork and whalebone, attached to her costume by rubber strings, whirled and swarmed around her dancing form. She had been the toast of San Francisco. When Remme met her she was at a horse auction at Marysville where she outbid him for the gray he had borrowed from the pasture. They had become friends and he had visited her in Marysville. Though he had admired her, he was wise enough to know that her temperament was too wild and unpredictable for the two of them to become more than friends. She was famous, loved the limelight, and he was a small cattle trader who was gone for months at a time on the trail.

As the gray pounded north through the flat land on the wagon trail to Red Bluff, Remme knew the easy part of his ride was behind him. The last of the day's light gradually disappeared and the horse beneath him lost its sharp outline. Shadows made the trail ahead obscure, but he refused to allow the

gray to slacken her pace, fully aware how dangerous it was to be running at full gallop as the twilight
deepened. An unseen small animal or bird seeking
a nesting place for the night could cross the trail,
collide with the gray, startle her and cause injury to
the horse.

With the light gone, the chances of the gray
stepping into a gopher hole were a hundred times
greater. Still, Remme could not let up. In his imagination he could see the Pacific Steamship
Columbia plowing through the ocean unimpeded
by nightfall. Every minute of speed was precious to
him if he was going to beat the *Columbia* to
Portland. There would be dozens of times on the
trail ahead when natural obstacles would reduce his
progress to a walk. But the boat wouldn't stop; it
would beat northward relentlessly mile after mile,
not dependent on horsepower and fighting spirit.

Remme refused to worry about the hazards he
could not see. He had strong faith that luck was
riding with him and a belief that if he let the horse
have her head, her own sense of the contours of the
earth beneath her feet, coupled with her night
vision, would prevent a spill. On he rode, his body
bent forward in the saddle, his mind and sinews
urging his mount forward.

It was near midnight, having covered more than 40 miles on the tireless gray, that the animal began to stumble and weave. She was dangerously winded and Remme, stiff and numb from hours in the saddle, stepped down to the ground and almost fell on his face. His feet were like blocks of wood, void of feeling. Gradually as he walked around the horse and stamped his boots and swung his arms circulation returned. When Remme could feel his toes again, he led the gray toward a campfire a hundred yards or so west of the trail.

A light drizzle was falling and a three-quarter moon sailed high in the murky sky between night clouds. Drawing closer to the fire, Remme shouted in a loud voice, "Hello the camp. Anybody home?"

The answer that came from a man he could not see froze Remme's blood:

"Show yourself against the firelight. Slow and easy now, unless you hanker for a lead belly ache!"

Holding the reins of his horse with one hand and with the other clearly in view, Remme stepped into the cheerful circle of light thrown by the fire, pulling the gray behind him. He turned his head as he heard a step and a tall man clad in buckskin with a white beard and flowing hair stationed himself in the half shadows just beyond the fire's glow. In his hands rested a rifle. The barrel was pointed straight at Remme's heart.

"Now, what do you want this time of night?"

"I'm chasing a horse thief," Remme said, thinking quickly that the idea he had struck on earlier would be a good explanation to strangers whose help he needed.

The bearded man lowered his rifle and glided into the firelight. Remme breathed easier and got a better look at the remarkable figure he had disturbed. Obviously a trapper, the man had the appearance of a person who spent most of his life outdoors and slept in his clothes. His buckskins were dirty brown, but neatly patched with lighter, newer squares of hide. He wore a red kerchief around his neck and moccasin boots that reached to below his knees. His face was hawkish with a wide mouth, hooked nose and fierce gray eyes. He looked sharply at Remme for a moment, then dropped to his knees, stirred the fire with a stick and poured coffee from a blackened pot into an empty clay cup. He held it out to Remme. "Here drink this."

As Remme thanked the trapper and sipped the strong brew he saw the man sizing up the gray which was trembling with fatigue, her head lowered.

"That's a fine horse you're riding. I'll swap you mine and get the best of the bargain."

"It's a borrowed horse," Remme said, "I'll have to swap back with you after I catch the man I'm after."

The trapper nodded. "I'll throw your saddle on my bay while you finish your coffee. How far ahead is the thief?"

Remme thought about the *Columbia's* ocean passage and shook his head, "Could be only a few hours if I'm lucky," he said.

The trapper grunted and patted the gray's neck then swiftly unstrapped Remme's saddle and carried it over his shoulder into the darkness beyond the fire. When he returned a few minutes later, he was leading an ugly, square-headed bay, a big, lumpy horse with knobby knees, a slight sway back, and high shoulders with bones that seemed to poke through the skin.

"He ain't much to look at, but he just keeps going. Feels like you're sitting in a rocking chair on his back, I call him Shorty 'cause he's so tall."

As Remme swallowed the last bitter taste of the trapper's coffee, he swung up to the saddle and took the reins from the trapper.

"Listen," the man said, "keep your eyes peeled for Injuns and watch your hair. They say the Klamaths have been ranging south of the Oregon border. And the Modocs are the worst of the lot." With that sparse advice, the trapper slapped Shorty on the rump and the big bay jumped into the night.

True to his word, the trapper's Shorty was a dream horse to ride. A powerful animal with a wide back and strong legs, he lunged north eagerly carrying his rider in a comfortable see-saw motion. Guided by Remme's light touch on the reins, Shorty fell into a long, loping rhythm that ate up the ground beneath his hooves.

Grateful though he was for the pleasant rocking of his horse, Remme had been in the saddle since noon—almost 13 hours. He was not tired so much as he was sleepy. The boost from the coffee he had drunk at the trapper's fire was fading and he reached into his pocket and found a handful of roasted coffee beans he had placed there. The bitter flavor of the beans bit into his tongue as he chewed them, but he swallowed the juice and soon felt more alert. Hungry, he broke a stick of dried beef jerky he took from a bundle in his saddle bags. The jerky was as hard as nails and in order for him to eat it he sucked on it until it softened in his mouth. A few minutes after he crunched the coffee beans and swallowed the jerky, Remme was refreshed. He felt more in tune with the thundering hooves of the bay.

As he broke through the night on Shorty with a cold wind rising from the west buffeting his body with sudden puffs of force, a new sound arched above the wind. Even though he had heard it many times in different places, it always reminded him of his own solitary life. He respected the watchers in the wilderness who traveled together with yellow eyes gleaming and called to one another in their high, sobbing voices. Shorty had veered slightly in his forward stride when the wolf howled, proving the big bay was also wary of the gray hunters.

Remme frowned, thinking the near presence of the wolves in the valley below the mountains might be a sign of something that did not bode well for him. If the critters were hunting in the low hills and valleys, it might be because the snow was too thick and deep higher up for them to find game. If that was the case in a hundred miles or so he could be facing winter passes blocked with snow. He wished now for a glimpse of the gray travelers. One look at the fur a wolf was wearing would tell him a tale of the weather. If the hairs were as long as his little finger, gray and thick as a rain cloud, he could probably count on bitter cold and heavy snow the higher he went.

It was at Towerhouse, five miles northwest of Whiskey Town an hour after dawn of the second day in the saddle, that Remme got his answer to the mountain weather. For seven hours he had ridden the willing bay hell-for-leather through the night. The big horse had seemed tireless as he carried Remme mile after mile through the darkness. All night the moon played hide and seek, darting behind clouds and hiding the wagon path Remme was following. Shorty had thundered on faithfully, flying through the patches of light and dark without hesitation. If Remme had admired the gray for her beauty and grace, he was impressed by the strength and endurance of the big bay. He promised himself to barter with the trapper for the horse when he came back from Oregon—if he won his race.

Now, Shorty was winded. Streaks and bubbles of lather painted his neck and shoulders like a film of soap. He stood with his head lowered behind the hitching rail in front of the livery stable in Clear Creek. He was gulping air and wheezing. Remme was proud of the hammer-headed bay and when he told the owner of the stable how the big, knobby horse had carried him almost 60 miles in seven hours, the hostler smoothed his hand over Shorty's back, clucked his tongue and said, "That's some horse. Wish he was yours to sell. I'll loan you a good mount and rest and feed this one. It'll cost you $5. I'll saddle Becky for you while you get breakfast."

Remme agreed, paid the man and trudged across the street to the Towerhouse.

As he walked he reflected that the stablemaster had not been surprised when he rode up and told his story about chasing a horse thief. He had accepted the lie as true and commented that the thief and stolen horse had not stopped at his stable. Remme was the only stranger he had seen in two days. Remme began to realize that the men to whom he told his tale swallowed his story because to them his pursuit of the thief was an example of frontier justice, and by helping Remme along the way with horses they were participating in the small drama of his chase.

Towerhouse was only three years old when Remme sat down in the dining room for a quick breakfast. The hotel was doing a brisk business mostly with miners who searched for gold in Clear Creek and the surrounding Trinity Mountain area. The hotel was known as the best roadhouse in California and Remme had taken meals in the dining hall many times. While he waited for his eggs and ham, he asked a man seated beside him at the long oak table what the weather was like in the mountains a few miles north. The man plainly was a miner. His hands were chapped and red from washing gravel taken from Clear Creek in a rocker and his boots and heavy coat wore tell-tale streaks of dried mud. Between bites of hot biscuit and sausage, the miner, who told Remme his name was Pearson, said, "It's been a bad one in the mountains to the north, I hear. If you're headin' that way, you'd better veer west as far as you can and keep to the valleys unless you want to get blown off your horse. The winds have been sweeping down the chute like a blast from the North Pole. Even down here, I've been chipping ice in the mornings all winter."

Remme thanked the miner for his information and tackled his eggs when they were delivered. He realized as he hurried through his breakfast that it was probably the last hot meal he would have for several days. A few miles north of Clear Creek, the wagon road ended and the tall mountains of pointed firs and pines rolled away to the north in a labyrinth of interlocking ranges, plunging canyons and craggy broken summits. There were forest trails known to men like himself, but as yet only a few wagons had creased the valley floors beyond the mining camps. The country ahead of him was wild, lonely and dangerous, with a thousand tricks to snare and trap an unwary horseman. It was no domain for breakneck riding, for whisking through the cloud-broken night hugging the neck of a fast horse. His progress would be much slower because it would be necessary for him to make time-consuming detours.

Sometimes the only way to overcome the mountains was to skirt them. Climbing them was impossible. At this time of year, some of the slopes were buried in twenty or thirty feet of snow, clinging to the hidden earth so precariously that a martin's cry would be enough to start a landslide. Remme knew the destruction the moving side of a mountain could cause. It was awesome. But skirting the mountains often meant swinging wide east or west through canyons that eventually would lead him to paths north. In some cases to gain a mile, he would have to ride five. But Remme had not underestimated the obstacles facing him when he started on his mad race.

Setting his jaw, he took the last sip of his coffee, paid for his breakfast and hurried across the street to the livery stable. He climbed on a medium black horse which the stablemaster claimed had a strong heart and clattered over the wooden bridge that spanned Clear Creek.

There were two routes roughly parallel that Remme could take north. Each one was hazardous; both of them had been made by miners exploring the creeks and rivers in the Trinity Creek wilderness. Remme decided on the western route because it was farther removed by a few miles from the influence of Mount Shasta whose snowy peaks reared 14,000 feet into the sky. Also, on the western trail there were more gold camps where he could trade horses with the hardy miners who braved the winter working their claims.

By late afternoon Remme put Weaverville behind him and was picking his way around snow-capped boulders and thick trees wearing a coat of white. He had discovered that Becky was a determined horse plodding patiently through snow drifts that were often chest high. As the afternoon wore on, Remme realized that the color of the sky was changing and the temperature was dropping rapidly. The air was becoming heavier and a leaden pall was spreading over everything. All the signs convinced him that a bad storm was brewing and he and Becky had no choice but to face it. He had to keep going because to wait for the storm to subside after it struck might mean a delay of a day or so while it blew itself out. Riding through a storm was not a safe decision; Remme knew that only too well. It was foolhardy and dangerous, but he had to weigh the fact that time was heavily against him in the uneven race he had accepted. Every minute counted. The *Steamship Columbia* had no serious obstacles to overcome, unless of course she encountered a storm at sea and had to run for shelter. He couldn't plan on such luck.

Even as he made his decision to push Becky forward, the wind suddenly picked up and drove at him with a sudden gust that held a sharp, freezing edge. Quickly, Remme reached into his saddle bags and pulled out the heavy woolen scarf he had packed. He folded the scarf lengthwise so that it resembled a long thick bandage and looped it over the crown of his hat and tied the ends tightly under his chin. He pulled the collar of his coat up to protect the back of his neck and fastened the top button in front. Now, with his hat pulled down close to his ears which were covered by the scarf and with his collar raised, the Frenchman looked like an old woman peeking from her shawl. Only his eyes, shaded by the lowered brim of his hat, peered out brightly taking in the slanting snow as it whipped at him and his horse.

Within minutes, Remme knew he was facing one of the most vicious storms of his life. He could only pray that he could push Becky through the worst of it. While he urged the game little horse to keep a constant trot, he let her have her head choosing the path forward. He had no choice. The snow was drilling him with thousands of needle pricks. It was blown by a wind that hugged the ground and screamed like an angry wildcat. It carried icy blasts that filled the air with biting particles fine as dust. It swooped in a horizontal stream peppering everything in its path with tiny pellets of frozen white fire. Soon, Remme could not see Becky's ears, so thick was the snow. With his head bowed, the main force of the wind struck the top of his hat and wobbled it on his head, trying to lift it from his scalp. Remme tightened the scarf under his chin feeling the crust of snow building up on the wool. In less than five minutes a layer of snow three inches deep covered the front of his coat. When he lifted his eyes to look ahead, the wind flung snow under the brim of his hat and with swift cold fingers searched cleverly for openings to his skin around the collar of his coat.

Becky swayed and stumbled and ran blindly, terrified by the thick howling snow that clogged her ears and filled the hollows of her eyes. She kept going, urged by the pressure of Remme's knees and her own growing panic to escape the blizzard.

It was when Becky started heaving and shaking

her head wildly that Remme pulled on the rains and dragged himself out of the saddle. Holding tightly to the reins, he pushed himself against the wind to reach Becky's head. The snow was like a thick cloud surrounding, drowning, covering everything that had a surface with layers of crystals and ice. Trees carried such a burden of snow that their shapes were lost; they were shaggy white mysteries, like miniature mountains sprouting from the ground. A sudden, brief let-up in the snow allowed Remme to see Becky's head in the white glare. What he glimpsed in that instant scared him and he reached for the knife in his belt. The worst of his fears had come true. Becky was suffocating, barely breathing through a mask of ice that covered her head from her muzzle to her ears. Her own hot breath condensing as moisture and blown back into her face by the icy wind had frozen to her hairy skin. Remme knew about killing ice. He had found cattle dead on the range, smothered in treacherous weather when their own warm breaths created the moisture that formed frozen hoods encasing their heads in glistening white sacks. Finally the ice closed off their nostrils and they suffocated.

Quickly, Remme cut breathing holes in the ice blocking Becky's nostrils and she snorted wildly, took several ragged breaths, shook herself and stamped her feet. Remme pulled her around so that her tail faced into the blowing wind, then, with extreme care he cut into the ice that had glazed over her eyes. When she could blink and moisture started running from the corners of her eyes, Remme opened his saddle bags and pulled out a spare cloth shirt. With the wind making puffs and billows in the fabric he succeeded, after two attempts, tying the arms of the shirt around Becky's neck. Then he pulled the body of the shirt over her eyes and nose. With a piece of rawhide string, he tied the shirttails closed beneath the horse's muzzle. When he finished, his shirt flapped and pulled around Becky's head, but it was secure protecting her face from the freezing wind. Eventually, the moisture from her lungs and breath would saturate the cloth and the shirt would freeze hard as a board. But Remme was betting that the cloth would not stick to the horse's skin. She could breath through the shirt even though her vision was blocked.

He wasn't concerned about Becky's hampered sight. She was a trail horse and answered to directions from the reins and the pressure of his knees in her ribs. He wiped the snow from his saddle and pulled himself on Becky's back, thankful that her actions had given him a warning of what was happening to her. He told himself he should have expected the wind to freeze the horse's breath. He should have examined her before she started having trouble.

Remme had no choice but to drive Becky once more into the cutting wind and snow. To stop meant death. Within minutes without shelter horse and rider would be blanketed with snow; body temperatures would drop and the end would be inevitable. He had a vague idea that they were still traveling north, but he could not have sworn to it. He plowed ahead on the black horse, brushing snow out of her mane, urging her on, rubbing his own nose and cheeks to keep the blood moving in his face. He listened to the voice of the crying wind for any change of tone or pitch that meant the storm was letting up.

It was an hour later when the storm died and the snow stopped. It was suddenly so quiet that Remme could hear Becky's soft breathing as she stood up to her chest in a snowdrift. Vapor and sweat converted to steam rose smoking from her hide.

Remme had to cut his shirt off of Becky's head. The cloth was embedded with particles of ice and horse hair. She nickered when he removed the frozen tail of his shirt from her eyes, then blinked and swung her head up and down as if to express her relief that she could see again. When he climbed back on his horse, one look at the snow scene that surrounded him told him how lucky he had been to survive the storm. If Becky had bolted when he had removed the ice mask from her head, as many horses would have done, he could have been lost in the storm. And, careful as he had been with his knife, he saw that he had cut the skin on the inside of the horse's left nostril when he freed her air passages of ice. The wound had bled and froze.

Remme patted Becky's neck affectionately and looked around him. As far as he could see snow blanketed the ground to a depth of three or four feet, high enough to come just under Becky's belly. Mountain shrubs like rabbit brush, and ocean spray—the sturdy plant that the Indians used as stock for their arrows—looked like huge foot stools slip-covered with snow. Then, suddenly the white world around him blazed as the sun broke free of the clouds and poured golden light on the carpet of snow. The glare was so fierce that for a moment Remme was blinded by the reflection. He threw up his arm to protect his eyes and Becky started back nervously. When Remme opened his eyes again there appeared, as if it had just been made, Mount Shasta, reaching into the sky like a white dream. There it stood, probably 80 miles away, forever distant, aloof, a shining pinnacle whose reaches no man had climbed. It commanded the four directions of the wind and beneath its covering of snow a volcanic heart of fire reached deep into the earth.

Remme had seen the mountain many times, but never had it appeared so grand and remote. Even as it blazed fiercely white against the blue of the sky, the sun went behind a cloud and the mountain receded into the horizon. It was still to be seen, but its outline was faint and dim.

A man who had spent most of his life in the wilderness, Remme was convinced that the sudden appearance of Mount Shasta was an omen of good fortune. He had witnessed some strange tricks of the weather in the wilderness but he did not judge an event as mysterious or odd, or as an act of God. Why something happened wasn't important. He couldn't control the sun or move the stars, but he could be grateful when nature favored him with a stroke of luck. Not only had Shasta cheered him after a grim night of shrieking snow and ice, but it stood in a vast field of featureless snow as his directional beacon. He knew the mountain was north-east of the trail to Trinity Creek. He couldn't be more than five miles from Cox's Store. There he could swap Becky for a fresh horse, catch a few hours of sleep and ride on. Despite his sense of urgency, he knew he had to sleep. He had to restore his strength. He had been awake almost 48 hours, and in the saddle for most of that time. His vision was playing tricks on him—spots that didn't exist swam in his eyes, the hairs on Becky's ears seemed much larger than they were, the horizon shifted when he tried to focus his eyes. He was jittery, nodding in the saddle, and his body, tough as it was, was aching with fatigue.

When Remme dismounted from his horse at Cox's Store, he staggered when he put his feet on the ground. Major Isaac Cox, a bearded man who operated the store on the south bank of the Trinity River, took one look at Remme, whom he knew—red eyed, with a two-day beard on his face—and guided him into the storeroom. There among canned goods, leather harness, shovels, gold pans, and sacks of cornmeal and flour, Remme sprawled and was asleep almost before his head touched the floor.

It was five hours later when Remme felt Cox's

hand on his arm. True to his word, Cox awakened
the Frenchman at 2:00 pm. Groggy, but refreshed,
Remme grunted his thanks to Cox, clumped
through the two-room store and outside scooped
up a double handful of snow and pushed his face
into it. When his skin began to tingle, Remme
dropped the melting snow, shook water from his
fingers and put his hat back on. He accepted a cup
of coffee from Cox who told Remme he had fed
Becky and transferred the saddle to a motley gray-
white horse Cox had taken in trade from a miner for
provisions.

"I've ridden him, Louis," he said. "And he's
sturdy. A gelding. Wants his own head. Stubborn.
Reminds me of you. Now, what's this story you told
me about chasing a horse thief?"

Remme had repeated his tale of chasing a horse
thief to Cox before he fell asleep. He had had to tell
the store owner something to cover his strange
request to be awakened in five hours with a fresh
horse waiting for him.

Spooning peaches into his mouth from a jar he
purchased from Cox, he enlarged his story, between
bites, of the imaginary horse thief. Taking in
Remme's dusty appearance, the horse lather stains
on his coat and pants, the circles under his eyes,

Cox said, "That must be some horse to chase a man as far as you've come. I hope you catch him."

Remme thanked Cox for his good wishes, then asked the question that had been burning in his mind, "What about the Indians?"

"Well, that's a different story," Cox said. "The Modocs have been raiding all along the frontier—along the Oregon border. I hear they've attacked villages and have taken slaves from the Shastas, the Pit Rivers, and the Paiutes. 'Course they've been doing that for a hundred years. If the man you're chasing is heading into Oregon, I hope for your sake he's steering clear of Tule Lake. There's been no wagon trains with settlers since early fall. But, heck, you probably know that the Modocs and some of the Klamaths have been killing whites near Bloody Point. And all winter, I hear, they've been stealing horses anywhere they can find them. Somebody's got to get a posse together and go after the devils like Ben Wright did back in 'Fifty-two."

Remme nodded his head. He remembered three years earlier hearing about the sole survivor of an Indian massacre who rode into Yreka with a grizzly tale. The Modocs had attacked a wagon train near a place that became famous as Bloody Point. The man who escaped with his life told of the slaughter

of sixty-four men, women and children. All of the
bodies had been horribly mutilated and scalped. An
armed posse of men had stormed out of the town
headed by Ben Wright, an Indian fighter who wore
his hair as long as any brave. By flaunting his shoulder length curls, he was making his scalp valuable
to the Indians as a battle trophy and he was proving
his own courage and daring. Remme, who wore his
own hair long, thought Wright was a reckless fool.
He knew the man who had become Indian agent
for the tribes that lived near the mouth of the Rogue
River in Oregon. He thought Wright's determination to make a target of himself for renegade
Indians was the kind of arrogance that endangered
the lives of the men who rode with him. One day
he'd pay for his bravado with his own scalp.

Remme knew that the hunting party from Yreka
headed by Wright tracked and killed several
Modocs, but the Indians continued to prey on settlers headed to Oregon and the Applegate Cutoff
into the Willamette Valley. The French Canadian
was fully aware that a lone horseman like himself
was a favorite target of roving bands of braves. One
of the games they loved to play was for one brave
with two horses to chase a solitary horseman. If the
man alone was mounted on a swift pony, the sport

was more fun because the brave had to switch horses on the run, finally overtaking the rider on the fresher exchange horse. The horseman was rarely left alive when the whole party of braves caught up with him and his Indian pursuer.

Remme dropped his empty peach jar into a wooden refuse barrel. "I'll watch my hair, Isaac," he said to the storekeeper, and thanked Cox for his information about the Modocs.

As Remme turned the gelding north from Cox's store, he knew he was moving into hostile country. In the next 150 miles the danger to himself from attack would increase tenfold. One of the reasons for that was that he was in mountain country, a rising land of volcanic peaks surrounded by white bark pines and red fir forests. A perfectly rounded cone, called Black Butte, composed of millions of small, black lava rocks thrust its domed peak more than a mile into the sky just southeast of his path. But due north of him was a wide stretch of open, treeless, gently rolling sage brush country, dotted with volcanic debris that had been scattered for miles when Shasta stirred to life in the past erupting with smoke and thunder and sending thousands of tons of red hot rocks into the valley below it. Putting two and two together, he had decided when he first saw the prairie-like land north and west of Mount Shasta years before, that the mountain's fiery lava had burned the area clear of trees. It was a land of cold cinders and sage brush. For a solitary traveler like himself, the miles of open space, where a horse and rider silhouetted against the sky stuck out like a sore thumb, were dangerous. There was no place to hide. A chase would be won by the rider with the fastest horse. And Remme knew when he reached Calahan's ranch less than 50 miles from where he was that he had to decide how to get across the wide stretch ending near the Oregon border. Dozens of unknown men had been run down by Indians who hunted the area for antelope and deer. They disappeared with only their bones to mark the places where they fell.

As Remme pushed the gelding north along a track where the snow was thinner on the ground, he thought about the heavy price the pioneers who came west paid for the land they were eager to settle. He had been a green young man when he saw his first covered wagon pull out of Saint Louis for the Oregon Trail. That had been sixteen years earlier. Since then waves of settlers had pointed their wagons west into country previously populated only by the free-ranging natives. The lives of the pioneers taken by the Indians to defend their land were negligible compared to the ones sacrificed to the hardships of the trail. Every mile west was an elongated graveyard for hundreds of men, women and children who did not survive.

Better than most frontiersmen, Remme understood the anger of the various Indian tribes that attacked covered wagons with pioneer families and lone riders whose horses would give braves who stole them new mobility and tribal recognition. Chief among the reasons for the wrath of the Modocs and the Klamaths was the fact that wagon trails ran through summer hunting grounds scaring the game away. Another bitter complaint was the diseases brought by the immigrants. They killed hundred of Indians. Whole villages were wiped out. But all of the Indian's bitterness could be summed up in one sentence: Their way of life was being threatened and the whites were responsible.

5

Trouble came for Remme not where he expected it, but shortly after he crossed the Oregon border. He had exchanged horses three more times, once at Calahan's ranch, again with a miner in Scott Valley, and in Yreka on the morning of his third day. There he borrowed a pony from Horsley and Brothers Mountain Express where he repeated his story of chasing a horse thief. Impressed by his determination and nerve, the men who operated the delivery service loaned him their fastest horse, a piebald, brown and gray with one white foot. Four hours later after crossing the open stretch of sage brush land he dreaded without challenge, the cold, weary French Canadian climbed the long snowy slope eleven miles north of where he forded the Klamath River. It was in the Siskiyou Mountains when he slid out of his saddle in front of a huge pile of smooth stones which was heaped in a triangular shape around a small oak tree. The tree's lower boughs had been cut away with an ax and part of the trunk that projected above the stones bore the curious mark of United States Surveyors. The tree and the stones around it marked the boundary line between California and Oregon territory.

Remme studied the surveyor's symbol cut deeply into the bark for a moment and sighed, "Thank God for Oregon." Then he kneeled in the snow on the bank of Hungry Creek nearby and cracked ice with the handle of his knife. He drank deeply and splashed the freezing water in his face. As he turned, refreshed, to mount his horse he saw them. Three Indian braves sat on their horses not 200 yards away. They were staring directly at him.

Remme had confronted Indians in the wilderness before. Sometimes they meant no harm, finding satisfaction in studying the habits of white men from a distance. They were like children curious about new neighbors. Often they were fascinated by items of clothing—belt buckles, suspenders, felt hats, women's bonnets—or even the texture of the skin on the face of white strangers. But something about these three spelled menace to Remme. Carefully, he mounted the piebald, swinging his right leg over the saddle in a quick, effortless motion, never taking his eyes off of the trio. He was not surprised when they did not move, but continued to sit on their horses, motionless, like figures carved out of wood, and stared at him. Staring a man down was an old trick of some Indians Remme had learned about years before. Often it was harmless, but equally often it was a deadly game whose rules were known only to the Indians. For them, it was a duel of wits to see who would make the first move. A frightened man who decided to run for it might be pursued by nothing more dangerous than laughter from the Indians, tickled that they had outwitted a white man. On the other hand, swift arrows might be launched at the back of the rider who bolted.

Remme wasn't sure which tribe the three Indians came from. Two of them wore buckskin shirts and pants, rawhide leggings, and blankets over their shoulders. They were bareheaded with their black hair divided in braids that fell on either side of their faces. The third brave was dressed in the same fashion except his buckskin shirt fell down to his thighs which were bare. His heavy leggings covered his skin up to his knees. Also, like the others, over his right shoulder hung a tightly strung bow and quiver with arrows. The horses on which the braves were mounted were small and shaggy, but looked fresh and spirited. As far as Remme could make out none of the three was armed with a rifle, although around their waists each of them wore a belt with a long knife attached. These men were a small hunting party. The question was was it wild game they were after, or the scalp of a solitary rider after they rode him down and took his horse and weapons?

Remme's decision to turn his horse and move slowly was based on his hunch that the longer he stayed the more determined the Indians would become to win the staring contest. Also the longer nothing happened, the longer the braves would have to work up their courage and decide that three against one, even if the one was armed with a rifle and pistol, were good odds. He was certain the braves were smart enough to figure out that the way to attack a man armed with guns was to separate and come at him from three different directions. One of them was bound to get through.

As Remme clucked to the piebald and turned his head north, he was aware that the Indians probably had a big advantage over him. The piebald was not fresh. He had carried Remme fifty miles and was almost played out. Maybe the dappled horse had another five miles in him, but he wasn't up to a lengthy chase.

For an hour Remme guided the piebald north, deeper and deeper and gradually higher up a mountain slope through crusty, day old snow that reached at times up to the chest of the pony. The Indians followed never decreasing the distance between them and Remme, but never allowing the gap to widen. All the while he moved forward with the Indians trailing behind, the back of Remme's neck tingled with the threat they represented. It took all of his self control to force himself not to turn anxiously in his saddle to see if the braves were creeping up on him—getting within arrow range of his back. Remme knew the situation had to change. Sooner or later the braves would lose patience and suddenly whoop with blood-curdling yells and plunge after him. The piebald was making it easier for the Indians to catch up by breaking trail for them.

It was after two hours of playing a deadly cat

and mouse game near the summit of a small mountain pass that the Indians broke loose. With shrill cries, they whipped their horses and tore up the snow in a wild charge.

Remme drove the piebald over the crest of the pass and down the other side of the mountain in a flurry of snow. Tired as he was, the horse headed down in a series of jumps that surprised Remme. Almost rabbit-like, the piebald sprang forward in leaps, pushing with the powerful muscles of his hind legs. The ride for Remme was like staying on a bucking horse. As the piebald's front feet struck the ground, spraying snow in small explosions, his hind feet were in the air and Remme was suspended momentarily above his saddle until the piebald's rear feet came to earth with a jarring thump. The French Canadian cattle trader managed to cast a glance backward only once during his wild descent and then he saw something that gave his heart a lift and chilled his blood at the same time. The brave wearing the long buckskin blouse and leggings had forged ahead of his companions who had stopped at the top of the hill. He was pushing his horse, like the piebald, in lunging jumps that covered about six feet at a time, seesawing down the slope in a cloud of snow. The fact that two of the Indians were hold-

ing back meant only one thing to Remme. The one
brave who came after him had decided the white
man was a worthy challenge to his manhood. He
would earn praise from his tribe by capturing the
man's horse and guns and taking his scalp unaided
by his friends. The prize was even worthier because
the brave was not armed like his opponent and
would have to catch the white man by wit and cun-
ning.

As Remme drove the piebald foot after foot up
the next steep mountain through the snow, sensing
the fatigue in the horse's legs, hearing his heavy
breathing, the faltering strength in his stride, he
noticed something in the air that disturbed him. It
was nothing he could name—a feeling, a tension, a
shimmering pressure that warned him of danger far
greater than the lone warrior who was coming after
him. When he understood what it was, he brought
the piebald to a halt and turned him so Remme
could see the top of the mountain far above hidden
in a cloud, and the deep bottom in the white valley
below. If he could have described the threatening
quality of the mountain that frightened him it was
like a quivering in the air before thunder strikes—as
if everything around him, the ice-smooth rock
faces, the snow-covered cedar trees, the short,

ragged pines, the deep snow blanket clinging to the mountain, was suspended and waiting. Remme thought about drawing his rifle and shooting at the brave to discourage him from coming up. But the loud cracking sound of the rifle would hasten what he knew was going to happen.

He started to yell to the Indian to turn around when he realized it was too late. At the last instant before the danger struck the brave's eyes popped open wide with fright when he felt the ground stir and shake. One moment, the Indian was mounted on his horse not 200 feet away from Remme and the next, still clinging to his pony with his legs, he and the animal started moving down hill rapidly, powered by a force that stripped snow from the side of the mountain like a sharp knife. The snow slide started just six feet below where Remme and the piebald stood. A huge wedge of snow 500 feet wide and five or six feet deep separated from the snow pack where Remme and his horse waited. It thundered and rumbled down the mountain like the tide rushing out, leaving a ragged gap that widened swiftly. Neither Remme nor the piebald dared to move. They were stunned by the avalanche and Remme was amazed to see the brave throw himself off of his horse as it sank. Face down, he landed and flung his arms outward in a swimming motion, trying to keep above the snow pouring in waves down the mountain. With a wild scream his pony fell on his back and was quickly drowned as the rushing snow piled over him creating a mound in the surface that disappeared in the flow. The avalanche swept the struggling Indian hundreds of yards down slope before Remme rode down the mountain. As he drew the piebald abreast of the Indian he saw the man was not deeply buried and he was not dead.

He had been stripped as naked as a skinned potato. Not a shred of his clothes remained and cuts and bruised covered his body. A cap of snow crowned his matted and snarled hair. He pulled himself to his feet standing up to his waist in snow and stared bitterly at Remme as if the avalanche was his fault. Remme rode away from the naked man awed that only six feet had separated him and his horse from the edge of the snow slide.

The tired piebald needed little encouragement from Remme to stumble ahead slowly. Both horse and rider had been going on nerve during the last two hours of the chase by the Indians. Remme decided the redskins had been from a band of Modocs that roamed between the Klamath and

Rogue rivers. They attacked settlers and horsemen riding alone, but they weren't as bad as the deadly and murderous bunch that roamed the Grave Creek hills further north. They were known to attack without warning from ambush. He had been lucky evading the three braves who had chased him, and his life seemed charmed to have been saved by a few feet from the avalanche that stripped the single Modoc bare and killed his horse. But Remme dared not trust his fate to a tired mount when he entered the Grave Creek region. As it was, he and the piebald were so exhausted that neither was alert to danger. Luckily, Jacksonville, Oregon was just a few miles away. There he would find oats for the horse and a place to sleep for himself. He had to sleep. His body craved rest.

Remme looked even worse than he felt. His sheepskin coat was spattered with mud, melted snow and horse lather stains. The warm white collar of his coat was bedraggled and gray. His shirt, pants and boots were speckled with grass, pine needles, and streaks of dirt thrown up by the hooves of the horses he had ridden. His hat looked as if it had been thrown in the mud, then stamped on. He could never remember being so tired in all of his life. He had been in the saddle for three and one half days with only five hours of sleep. That was when he curled up on the floor of Isaac Cox's storeroom. All of that time his tough body had been hammered mile after mile by the jarring hoofbeats of the horses he rode. His muscles ached from the beating they had received. During the eighty hours since he had left Sacramento he had munched coffee beans, chewed on dried jerky and hard biscuits and had eaten only two hot meals, one at Clear Creek and one at Yreka. The pursuit by the Modocs had tired him more than he was willing to admit. As the piebald jogged along wearily, Remme's eyes kept falling shut. Unconsciously, his body slumped and his head fell forward on his chest. Twice in an hour he woke with a start, shaken that the piebald was not moving. The horse halted when he felt the reins go slack and the man in the saddle released control.

Each time this happened, Remme awoke, shook himself like a wet dog shedding water, looked around to get his bearings, then urged the piebald into a trot. He finally managed to force his eyes open by thinking about the *Steamship Columbia.* Where was she now? he wondered, and with a sinking feeling estimated that she must be plowing ahead of him on a direct line paralleling the rugged

Oregon coast.

As he topped a rise and spotted the mining settlement of Jacksonville, he swore to himself he would not let his anxiety about the progress of the *Columbia* defeat him. It took six days for the boat to sail between San Francisco and Portland. The captain of the ship didn't know a crazy Frenchman was racing his craft to Portland. He had no urgent reason to pour on the steam or break any records. If the *Columbia* was on schedule, Remme guessed the position of the boat was slightly in advance of him, probably ten miles out on a line with the mouth of the Rogue River. If that was the case, he still had a chance. The worst of the snow country was behind him, although there were still fifty miles of mountainous terrain he had to cross before he reached the south end of the Willamette Valley.

When Remme stepped off the piebald in Jacksonville, he handed the reins to the hostler at the livery stable and said, "I'm bushed. Been chasing a horse thief and I'm all in. Give my horse oats, brush him down and let him rest. He deserves it. I've got to sleep. Do you have a stall with clean hay?"

"We got a hotel here. Just around the corner," the hostler said.

"Too tired to walk that far," Remme said. "Here's five dollars to care for the horse. Will you wake me in an hour and find me a fresh horse? A fast one?"

"Sure," the man said, pocketing the money. "Take the fifth stall. It's clean."

Remme untied the blanket roll on his saddle, trudged to the empty stall and spread his blanket on the hay. He curled up and was asleep in seconds. He didn't hear the stablemaster grumble to himself, "Never heard of a man who'd sleep on hay when he could rent a hotel bed."

Remme rode southeast for almost two hours before he reached the banks of the Rogue River. The horse he rode, furnished by the stablemaster in Jacksonville, was an eager black filly only four years old. Her name was Idaho and she was the smallest of the horses Remme had bought or borrowed. The stablemaster claimed she loved to run and could outdistance many bigger horses.

When the stablemaster woke him, Remme had washed his face in the horse trough, then decided that he'd better take a hot meal at the Jacksonville Hotel. It might be three days before he'd be able to sit at a table with food prepared in a kitchen to fill his stomach. After steak and potatoes, biscuits, beans, and a piece of apple pie and three cups of coffee, Remme was ready for the next stage of his journey. With an hour of sleep and a solid meal under his belt he felt like a new man as he paid for his meal and asked the cook/waitress, a jolly, plump woman, what was the news about the Indians.

She smiled at Remme, wiping her hands on her apron and said, "Plenty of them." Then she threw back her head and laughed with a funny screeching sound.

A few minutes later when the stablemaster asked Remme if Crazy Annie had fed him well, Remme said, "Why do they call her that?"

"Lost her whole family to Indians up around the Dardanelles," the man said. "Hasn't been right in the head since then, but she can sure cook."

With Remme on her back, Idaho started out quickly and proved she liked to run. She also demonstrated that she was steady and didn't startle easy when Remme was guiding her down a seldom used trail near Elk Mountain. It was early afternoon, the day sunny and spikes of new Indian grass were just beginning to bloom. The sight of the pale yellow pompoms in a meadow cheered Remme. He was riding into spring, even though there were patches of snow on the ground and higher up snow and ice still lay frozen on the peaks. As he steered Idaho past a thicket of stunted hemlock, there was a thrashing in the lower branches and the horse side-stepped smartly and froze. A blue grouse, plump as a setting hen, hopped out from beneath the tree and strutted in a circle eyeing Remme and Idaho, then boldly fluttered back into hiding.

Remme patted Idaho's neck and laughed at the hen. For some reason she reminded him of the laughing cook in Jacksonville who had lost touch with reality after her family had been massacred.

It was going to be tricky for Remme to stay in the saddle crossing the Rogue River on Idaho. Swift and cold, lapping both banks with the overflow from melting mountain snow, the river was wild, swift and noisy. It was strong enough to tear a man off his horse and tumble animal and rider like stones along its sandy bottom. The voice of the Rogue was a steady roar as Remme searched upstream for a shallow break in the current. He had to cross the river; he couldn't afford to spend the time to scout for miles up and down to find the safest place to make his entry. The best place he saw to ford was a flat bar in the middle that divided the river with an island. Thickets of willows grew on the island and a tall gray crane was standing on one leg. On both sides of the island water started shallow and ran deep. Remme had no choice but to jump Idaho into the flow above the island, counting on her to swim against the current and scramble onto the island as the river swept her close to the bar.

Idaho seemed to know exactly what was expected of her as Remme turned her to face the river with a head start of about 200 feet. When he flicked the reins and nudged her with his heels, she sprang forward eagerly. She was flying, and with a final push of her strong hind legs she sailed off the bank, brushing through tall grass, and splashed into the water with a huge, shocking spray about fifteen feet out into the river. Despite his preparation, Remme was unseated as Idaho sank, then came blowing to the surface swimming furiously to buck the strong flow of the Rogue. Though he was floating free of his horse, Remme did not relinquish his grip on the pommel of his saddle. With his head above the water, he watched as the strong, powerful little horse churned the water with her legs, going against the downstream drag of the current. As Idaho's front hooves touched the island, she pulled herself out of the clinging water with a sudden lurch and heave and stood shaking herself, spraying the air with a shower of drops. The gray crane, startled, hopped twice, flapped his long wings and took to the air, disgruntled that he had been disturbed.

Remme didn't bother emptying his boots. Holding Idaho's reins and giving her an encouraging pat, he walked to the far side of the island with the horse. The distance to the bank was about 300 yards. The water ran in streams and steam rose from his wet clothes in the cold air as he climbed aboard Idaho and barely touched the reins before she was in the water swimming. The current, less vicious on the lee side of the island, deposited horse and rider about and eighth of a mile downstream.

Remme took the time to wring out his shirt and squeeze as much water from his coat as he could. Once again he checked the slim leather case inside the oilskin pouch in which he carried his certificate of deposit from Adams Express. It was still dry when he opened the flap.

6

Five hours after Remme crossed the Rogue
River, he was plodding carefully through a mountain pass with fog laying in high patches of ground-
hugging gray clouds. They towered above the firs,
blocking portions of his trail, decorating the trees
with long, wispy beards. He and Idaho drifted
through the thick, clinging mist like ghosts appear-
ing and disappearing. It was when they emerged
from a long, dense layer of fog, clammy with moisture that goose-pimpled Remme's skin, that the
shots came. He felt the whipping breeze of bullets
whizzing past his head at the same moment he
heard the crack of rifles.

Remme kicked Idaho in the ribs, threw a hasty glance over his shoulder, and leaned against the horse's neck as the eager pony jumped into a racing run. As Idaho headed down between natural breaks in the trees, Remme heard the thunder of horses following and Indian voices raised in excitement. Unmistakable was the blood-thirsty ring in the chilling yells of the pursuers. They were no casual hunting party that had discovered a lone rider by chance and decided to play a game of chase with him. These were riders of vengeance whose murderous intent was to overtake Remme quickly, kill him, take his scalp as a trophy and leave his body for the turkey buzzards. Remme had eluded Indians more than once during his years on the frontier, but something told him that this encounter was the most dangerous of all. He was determined not to panic as he lay close to Idaho's neck with her flying mane brushing his right cheek. By molding his body as close to his running horse as possible, he was reducing the target area his back presented to the Indian's bullets. As if to emphasize his thought, rifles cracked again and Remme felt something pluck at his coat sleeve. A bullet made a hole in the hide of his sheepskin, barely missing his skin. He hunched lower on Idaho's back urging her to run faster as she flew down the mountain.

No sooner did Remme discover how close the single bullet had come to reaching its mark than several more shots sounded closer behind him. Like angry bees, lead whizzed by him picking at his clothes and cutting hairs from Idaho's flying mane. He cast a look to his rear and saw the Indians pressing closer. He swallowed hard as he glimpsed the grim faces, painted with bars and stripes, The heat of the chase was reflected in the narrowed eyes of the warriors and they glittered with hostility.

Gazing ahead of his horse, reading the terrain for deadly obstacles that could prove as fatal as any bullet if Idaho were to misjudge her footing, Remme thought of something his grandfather had once said to him. "Never forget, some Remmes are more dangerous when they are almost dead."

He didn't understand what his grandfather meant until the old man told him about his narrow escapes while fighting against the British alongside the treacherous Hurons who tried to kill him. Once, they left him for dead with a terrible scalp wound. Found at last by French soldiers, he heard one of them say, "This one's too far gone to bother with."

"Like hell I am," Paul Remme said. He lived to fight again and raise a family. There had been

Remmes fighting Indians and working the land since 1740.

Now, like his grandfather, Remme was not going to let the angry Indians of the band chasing him frighten him into making a mistake. He cast another glance over his shoulder and made out five men on horses. All of them were armed with rifles and they were gaining. He had to think of something quickly to give himself an edge. Idaho was running straight out, but she couldn't keep the pace going very long. Strong-hearted as she was, no horse her size had the stamina for a drawn-out chase, and the Indians were pushing hard. That was when Remme spotted the rocky area ahead and to the east of the path Idaho was taking. The decision he made took only a moment, yet it was filled with the clear knowledge of the risk he was taking with his own life to save it, and the damage he was exposing his horse to. It was a gamble that could win the race for him, or it could be the last mistake he ever made.

What he had seen ahead of him was the disguised result of what nature had done thousands of years earlier. The whole Cascade range—six hundred miles of it—a mountain wall stretching from Canada to northern California—was the result of

volcanos erupting, lifting and forming a long ridge
of peaks. Though Remme was unaware of the geo-
logical history of the mountains, he knew there
were scattered areas where lava rocks had boiled
out of the mountains long ago to cool and form beds
of stone like sharp teeth rising from the earth. There
were some areas to the east of him where vast fields
of lava spread for miles over mountains and
prairies. Eventually, in some areas the forests
roasted by the hot lava fires grew back, taking root
in chinks in the lava. As time went by more soil
formed and spread over the lava rocks. Plants and
bushes grew, and in some places they concealed the
protruding teeth. But the jagged stones were still
there, potent and deadly, more vicious because they
lay in wait to shred the feet or hooves of any animal
unwise enough to trod the ground that barely covered them.

The area where Remme directed Idaho was
grassed over and there were brave splashes of
Indian paintbrush, clumps of rabbit brush and dust-
colored sagebrush growing in the shade of cedar
and fir trees. Patches of snow lay thinly on the
ground. Remme winced as he urged Idaho into the
hidden lava teeth and heard her squeal with pain.
Brave horse, she clattered on, stumbling, dodging,

dancing and swerving to avoid the cruel cutting edges of the rocks. She penetrated almost half a mile into the lava rock region before Remme brought her to a halt.

Howls of rage and disappointment from the Indians was accompanied by furious rifle fire from them as their horses encountered the rocks. Unable to reach Remme by horseback without maiming the feet of their unshod ponies, three of the warriors dismounted and started to cautiously follow Remme on foot. Remme was waiting for them. Pulling Idaho behind a tree for partial protection, he threw himself off his horse, yanking his rifle from its sling as his feet touched the ground. He fired rapidly at the three in the distance, levering a fresh shell into the firing chamber of his rifle as fast as he jacked a smoking one out. He saw one of the Indians fall back and grab his leg. His companions lifted him quickly and retreated. Remme continued to fire until finally, the small band of Indians withdrew. He remained crouched beside the tree for half an hour, scanning every possible approach to his position before he placed his rifle in its sling and bent to examine Idaho's hooves.

What he saw drew a deep breath of regret from him and he shook his head sadly. Idaho was standing on three feet, holding her left front foot off of the ground. When Remme examined it carefully, he saw the long deep tear in the skin with blood running down her leg from above the fetlock into the the top of the hoof. A rock had sliced her leg as wickedly as a knife, cutting through the tendon. She had no control over her hoof. The tough sinew connecting it to the muscle was severed.

The brave little pony had saved Remme's life at the expense of her own. She was helpless; she could only move by hobbling. And without the use of her wounded leg, she would be easy prey for the wolves. Remme knew what he had to do as he unstrapped his saddle and his saddle blanket from Idaho's back. He ran his hand affectionately over her soft muzzle and when she nickered, he felt miserable and couldn't force himself to look into her trusting brown eyes. He drew his pistol quickly, pointed the barrel beneath her left ear and pulled the trigger. Her legs crumpled and she fell in a motionless heap even as the flat bark of the pistol died away. Leaving the saddle and blanket where they lay, Remme slung his saddle bags and bedroll over his shoulder, tucked his rifle beneath his arm, and stepped away from the fallen horse, knowing that he would remember her sacrifice whenever he thought of the bravest ponies he had ever ridden.

As he trudged ahead over the submerged lava carefully picking his way to avoid the sharp stone teeth, he thought about the wooden hobby horse his father made for him when he was five years old. It was remarkable, he thought, as he visualized the shiny horse balancing on its rockers, how he could actually smell the last coat of varnish his father had brushed on the smooth wood. The sharp, tangy odor was a memory he always associated with Christmas, and oranges, hot minced pie, turkey and cider, the green tree, fragrant and decorated with precious ornaments his grandmother had brought to the new world from France.

Clever with his hands, his father had carved the pony out of a solid piece of walnut. Lovingly, he fashioned a flying mane on the horse, arched his neck and stretched his legs so that the spirited wooden animal appeared to be running at full stride. With his red painted saddle, eyes of brown glass, stirrups and reins of real leather, Remme felt grown up when he mounted his steed and rode away in his imagination to explore the forest and hills surrounding his father's farm. Remme's pride and attachment to his hobby horse was transferred later to the favorite horses he encountered after he left home and learned to become an expert horse handler. He realized with surprise and a feeling of sadness as he broke free of the lava-toothed region, that Idaho had reminded him of his first horse, his swift hobby horse, which was probably gathering dust now in the wood shed of his father's farm in Quebec.

It had begun to snow as Remme started down a long sloping incline to a broad valley. He had walked about two miles and thought he was somewhere near the Dardanelles. As the snow quickened, he felt a sense of panic. He had no idea how many hours of trudging he had to do before he found another horse. His sense of time passing, leaving him behind, the *Steamship Columbia* sailing far ahead of him, plunged him into a black feeling of loss. Had not his whole venture been a foolish escapade? What had made him think that he could do what few men would have dared to try? Piercing the unforgiving winter wilderness of the Cascades was madness! Even the great mountain men, Levi Scott, Joe Meek, the Applegate brothers, who blazed the Southern Immigrant Trail, would have shunned the idea of winning an overland race against a steamship whose only hindrance was the time it took to sail from San Francisco to

Portland, Oregon. He had been extravagant with the strength of the horses he rode, finally killing one, all because of an impossible task. All because of his pride, his arrogance—his belief that he could do what other men would have described as crazy.

As the snow fell more quickly, thickening, sticking to his sheepskin coat, piling a crust on the brim of his hat, saddlebags and bedroll, Remme reached the lowest point of his life. He was dead tired, every muscle in his body throbbed; his head pounded like a drum, swelling and beating inside his ears. His legs were leaden and unsteady as his feet slipped on the new snow, his boots scuffing up small waves of the white. When he lost his footing, slipped and fell, his chin skidding like a small plow in the snow, he lay still. The skin on his hands burned with the cold; his clothes, still undried and clinging from the dunking he got when he and Idaho swam the Rogue, were clammy and smelled rankly of horse sweat and mildew and his own unwashed body.

He was far behind the schedule he had imposed on himself to beat the *Columbia.* As he lay wondering bleakly about his future, about how unfair life was, he suddenly heard his grandfather's stormy voice in his mind. "Get up from there! Get on your feet! Shame on you for thinking about quitting. Remmes don't give in!"

If he hadn't known better, Remme could have sworn his grandfather was standing over him shouting in his ear. He pushed himself up on his knees, looked around him and saw nothing but the dark shape of trees and the falling snow. He shouldered his saddlebags and bedroll and started walking again. His grandfather's disappointment had been so sharp, his commands so clear, that his words still echoed in Remme's mind: "Remmes don't give in."

As he trudged through the slanting waves of snow, Remme could not shake off the strong sensation that the old man's voice from the past had reached him, not from his mind, but from beyond Paul Remme's grave. It was a strange, haunting and comforting feeling. He felt ashamed that even for a few minutes he had given in to the idea of defeat. He had to go on. He had to make up the time he'd lost as a result of the Indian ambush that had cost Idaho's life and had stolen precious time from him. He had come almost 400 miles. He couldn't give up now. He had to play the hand he had dealt to himself to the bitter end.

The snow was mixed with rain as the bedraggled cattle trader topped a rise on a hill several miles later and saw dimly in a valley ahead a farmhouse with smoke rising from a chimney. There was a barn and animals in the barnyard surrounded by wooden fences. He heaved a sigh of relief and headed down into the valley. It was late in the afternoon, the snow transformed into a wavering line of insistent, icy rain that chilled him to the bone when he stopped a few yards from the front porch of the farmhouse and shouted "Hello!"

The sight he presented to anyone observing him was that of a dirty, bowed figure whose pale, drawn face was surrounded by a scruffy, four-day growth of hair bristling with drops of rain. His eyes were bloodshot and had a wild look; his arms trembled from the chilblains—a result of exposure to cold and damp from hours on end. And he swayed slightly from the dizziness that overcame him from time to time. His trousers and boots were muddy and shapeless. His sheepskin looked like it had been dragged in snow and mud behind a wagon for several miles. Unknown to Remme were three long bullet tears from Indian rifles in the greasy collar of his coat.

What Remme could not known as he waited for the door of the farmhouse to open was information about the *Columbia's* progress that would have cheered him beyond words. Because of Indian troubles, the steamship was carrying two companies of soldiers from San Francisco, as well as supplies to reinforce the army posts on Humbolt Bay in Northern California and at the army fort at Gardner located at the mouth of the Umpqua River in Oregon. The boat was delayed several hours to unload men and horses. About the time Remme was buying a strong horse from a stout Irish farmer named Kavanaugh who welcomed the cattle trader into his house when he heard him call, the *Columbia's* Captain Dall was aiming his steamship out to sea again. He had disembarked the last of the soldiers in Oregon. Remme was ahead of the steamship— but only by a few miles!

Kavanaugh was a big, cheerful man who promised Remme that the horse he was willing to sell for $80 was an even-tempered plodder. He was certainly no bolt of lightning like the horse Remme lost to the Shasta Indians. "Sasties is what they was," Kavanaugh said, using the frontier slang word for the tribe which had been named after the great mountain in California. The horse Remme bought from the cheerful farmer was a big, whitish animal with a Roman nose and huge feet from a Percheron ancestor. Whitey stood 16 hands high, was broad in the shoulders and had been trained to the plow.

"Ain't nothin' fancy about him," Kavanaugh said, "but he'll getcha where you're goin'. You may have to pester him some to make him stretch his legs but he's steady."

The shrewd farmer agreed to part with a dusty saddle covered with cobwebs that hung in the barn. It had seen better days but with a blanket thrown into the bargain it suited Remme and he agreed to pay $10 for it. Before Mrs. Kavanaugh would allow Remme to depart, she insisted that he eat a thick meatloaf sandwich. He consumed it gratefully, standing next to a hot potbellied iron stove that drove evil smelling steam from his wet clothes. Noting his pale face, Mrs. Kavanaugh placed the back of her hand against his forehead, then clucked her tongue and busied herself with hot water and two small jars. From one she took bark of the chokeberry tree and from the other needles of Douglas fir. She boiled the concoction and forced Remme to drink it. Bitter to the taste, but savory to smell, Remme obediently swallowed the brew and was surprised when a few minutes later the chills that had been trembling his body disappeared.

Kavanaugh had been watching and smiling as

his wife ministered to the pale, determined stranger who was chasing a horse thief. He chuckled to Remme and said, "Best cold remedy there is. Ma got it from an Indian woman over near Gold Hill. She swears by it. Sure makes me feel better when I get to ailing."

Darkness was closing in when Remme left the Kavanaugh farm and faced the long, wet night ahead of him on a broad-backed horse that slowed into a bone-jarring trot whenever he thought Remme wasn't paying attention. But the animal's stubbornness was endurable to Remme because Whitey demonstrated remarkable strength. The horse would need it to get Remme over the mudded Indian trail they were following. There was no more than a trace of it in the darkness.

While Remme was certain that he had put the threat of Indians and mountain snow behind him, the obstacle facing him now until he reached

Portland was drenching rain. In the wet months of early spring in western Oregon, the land became a giant sponge that soaked up water in every pore and cell. Time after time, immigrants had been stranded by thick, relentless rains that formed walls of descending water. Every blade of grass, crevice in the earth, curved leaf, nook and hollow was filled to overflowing with the drainage from the skies. Men and women confined to frontier cabins learned to hate the insidious rain that filled every ditch, weighted every plant and tree and invaded every human crevice that presented a dimple for water to find. Tables, chairs, doorframes and windows swelled with the insistent moisture. Tempers flared or people became cranky and morose. Settlers in wagons had been stranded for days at a time in driving rain that created shallow rivers and lakes on the ground and released the earth on hillsides to flow down in thick mud slides, like curdled molasses. A half a dozen rain-glutted rivers whose banks could be awash with overflow stood between Remme and his final objective, Portland.

Still, he forced the big horse to plod at a steady lope north, his hooves a sodden drumbeat on the flooded ground as he drove through the slanting wet. Soaked to his skin, Remme was grateful for small blessings. One was his durable hat that acted as a barrier to the descending drops. The wide brim of the sturdy felt had soaked up so much moisture that it flopped over Remme's forehead and the beat of the rain was like a constant roar in his ears. But the portion of the brim extending over his collar, also bent with moisture, protected his neck and carried the water pouring off the crown past his coat collar. If there was one thing Remme hated it was water trickling down the back of his neck.

About midnight in a gray curtain of persistent rain, Remme pulled Whitey to a halt, dismounted and stamped his deadened legs to return the circulation. He was famished and removed a jar of peaches from his saddlebags. In the downpour, he screwed the lid open and drank the sweet juice in big gulps, then ate the peach halves and realized how hungry he was. He chewed on a piece of tough beef jerky as he climbed back into the saddle heading into the dark side of dawn.

In the miles between midnight and daybreak the rain-blown rider thought again about his grandfather whose angry voice had raised him from the snow. He could picture the sharp face of the old man and wondered if, like his grandson, Paul Remme had ever had a moment of terrible weakness when he had survived the cold breath of death and lost faith in himself temporarily? His grandfather had believed that men and women who exercised self discipline could accomplish virtually anything. Had he ever seriously doubted himself? Of course, he had, Remme realized, or he wouldn't have understood the weakness in another man. Somehow understanding that about his grandfather made him feel better, stronger.

Sun-up found Remme on the banks of the Umpqua River near Roseburg. It was his fourth day in the saddle. The rain had stopped and a golden radiance drew miniature rainbows and sparks of light from dozens of puddles in the grass. He smiled when he saw a new spider web hanging between two bushes. It was a reliable weather sign that clear skies had replaced the rain. Though the river was high and dangerous to cross—a torrent of brown water carrying uprooted trees, bushes, shrubs and small dead animals—Remme's passage on Whitey was made much easier when he discovered a fir tree that lay across the Umpqua like a fallen giant. The big fir had toppled when its deep roots had been undermined by the swollen river digging away the bank where it had stood. The barrier formed by the fallen tree created a lake on the upstream side of the fir. It was a boon to Remme who held on to Whitey as the horse swam across. When the big horse pulled himself up onto the muddy bank, he shook himself, spraying Remme with water, mud and leaves. Drenched to the skin from the river crossing, his clothes draining brown water and drippy mud into his boots, Remme was beyond worrying about the condition of his garments. Steady rains for hours on end had made a sodden mess of his shirt, pants and coat, and his skin beneath the wet layers was puckered and wrinkled like a chicken whose feathers are wilted.

Early afternoon found Remme at the sturdy fir-shaded house of Jesse Applegate in the Yoncalla valley. He had met Applegate once before, but wasn't sure the Oregon trailblazer would remember him. He was riding a sorrel, a lazy horse he had exchanged for Whitey with a farmer, Levi Knott, a few miles from where Whitey had taken him across the Umpqua. As he dismounted in Applegate's yard, part of Remme's saddle came with him. It simply fell apart. He looked at the tangled leather in a heap at his feet and was not surprised. It was an old saddle, thin, brittle with age, not well made to begin with. The rawhide stitching that attached the left stirrup to the saddle frame had frayed and torn. The

$10 he had paid the farmer Kavanaugh for the
saddle had been too much money. But he had not
had a choice. He bent to pick up the fallen stirrup
and leg guard when Jesse Applegate opened the
door to his rambling cabin.

"Saddle trouble I see," he said with a smile.
"Isn't that Levi Knott's sorry old sorrel?"

Before Remme could answer, Applegate
observed, "You look like a man who's come a long
way in a short time. Coffee's on the stove and I'm
sure Cindy can find something to eat." He beck-
oned Remme to follow him and the cattle trader
nodded, trying to brush some of the mud off of his
clothes before he stepped through the door.

Compared to the cabins of most frontier settlers
the Applegate house was a miracle to Remme. A
warm, inviting smell of cinnamon and apples came
from the kitchen as the cattle trader stood self-con-
sciously in front of the fireplace warming his hands.
He was more aware of his coarse, dirty sheepskin,
muddy boots, damp shirt and pants and bristly
whiskers in the house where hooked rugs decorated
the stained and polished firwood floors and pictures
of Applegates hung from the cedar-faced walls.

When Applegate handed Remme a mug of hot
coffee, the Frenchman tried to apologize for his

appearance with a gesture, but Applegate put him at ease with the comment, "Cindy has some cinnamon bread baking and we'll have some when it's out of the oven."

Applegate frowned. "I'm trying to remember where I've met you."

Remme smiled, "I sold you some cows three years ago."

His face brightening, Applegate grinned. "Of course, you're the Frenchman."

The two men exchanged memories for a few minutes, then Applegate said, "From your appearance, you've had a hard ride. My guess is that you want to borrow a horse?"

Remme paused for a moment before he decided how to answer. Applegate was far different from the men with whom he had exchanged horses so far. This was the scout, turned farmer, whose name was respected all over Oregon. Thousands of men and women entered Oregon Territory in ox-drawn covered wagons following the immigrant trail that Applegate and Levi Scott had discovered at a terrible price to themselves. Separated from their families for months at a time, unpaid for their labors, the two had fought freezing weather, the terrible white winds of the Siskiyous, Indian attacks and brutal, punishing physical labor in the wilderness to map a trail immigrants could follow into the promised land. Remme had traveled over part of the trail—the Applegate Cutoff—when he rode into Oregon.

Now, he decided to tell Applegate the truth about his mad race to Portland. Somehow, the idea of asking the man to believe the lie about chasing a horse thief was wrong. When he explained why he was in a hurry and how far he had come, Applegate was astonished.

"My God, man," he said, "what you've done is impossible. All the way from Sacramento in four days! And you came through the Bobtail Mountains this time of year? You're lucky to be alive."

Applegate shook his head and looked hard at Remme as if observing for the first time a remarkable quality he had missed in the character of the man who warmed himself in front of the fireplace.

"Well, we've got to get you moving," he said. "You've got a long way to go." Then he added, "A lot of people in Portland are going to be hurt when Adams Express closes after the *Columbia* docks." He looked Remme squarely in the eyes and said, "I hope you make it. I can help by giving you the names of men who know me in the Willamette

Valley. They will trade horses with you—no questions asked. Just tell 'em Jesse sent you."

Applegate insisted that Remme drink a second cup of coffee and eat a big piece of Cynthia Applegate's fresh-baked bread while he placed a saddle on one of his favorite horses. He told Remme he could pay for the saddle and horse when he came back.

The trail Remme took north seated on Applegate's mare in a saddle that was strong and firmly made was a boggy trail that sucked at the hooves of the horse. Clinging like glue, the mud was a foot deep in some stretches forming thick mud pies around the mare's hooves. She skidded and slithered and threw clods of dirt that peppered Remme's pants and his saddle with mudballs. Soon, the front of his clothes, from the toes of his boots to his belt, was studded with mud that hardened into a thick layer. It wasn't until late afternoon that the laboring mare finally escaped the quagmires and mud traps and broke into the clear. That same night as Remme descended out of the hills into the main Willamette Valley the stars came out to speckle the sky with diamonds. Under the spangled sky, he pressed his horse with urgent prodding and breathed deeply the sweet odors of balsam and the curiously bittersweet tang of spring oak and madrona borne to him on the wind.

Though dead tired, his eyes drooping with fatigue, he forced himself to stay awake, sometimes by pinching the skin on his arms with his fingers. Another way he kept awake was to imagine that he was being chased by the Indians he had escaped on Idaho's back. Despite his best intentions, twice before dawn he fell asleep and woke with a start, sliding precariously sideways in the saddle—the falling sensation warning him at the last moment.

Near daybreak of the fifth day of his race to save his gold, Remme galloped through the muddy streets of the little settlement of Eugene City, then a dozen miles more to the farm of John Milliron. Applegate's name was like a password. Milliron appraised the Frenchman approvingly with his eyes and said, "The wife's got breakfast on the table. Eat while I put your saddle on a fresh horse."

Twenty minutes later, still munching a biscuit, Remme waved to Milliron and clattered out of the farmer's yard.

All that day, Remme continued to ride, his tough body jarring in a steady, weary rhythm of hoof beats and aching fatigue. Despite the fact that since he began his journey he had only closed his eyes for six hours, he was beyond sleep. His face was flushed; there was a fever in his eyes and his mouth and chin were chaffed from the constant wind. It was toward afternoon that Remme came within sight of the snow-covered peaks of the Cascade Range. All during his trip he had kept the rugged mountains east of him. Now, their appearance on the far horizon meant that he was within striking distance of Portland. The city lay west of the Cascades. He was close to his objective and he could not repress a thrill of satisfaction as he remembered Applegate's words: "What you've done is impossible." But even as Remme's optimism lifted his spirits, doubt undermined his mood. Where was the *Columbia?* Had she turned east from her northerly course to cross the bar where the powerful Columbia River met the surging Pacific Ocean? If the steamship already had entered the river heading upstream to Portland, then pray she had to make some stops before she finally dropped anchor in the city that lay on the banks of the Willamette River. It was the last river Remme had to cross to arrive in Portland.

The following morning, dawn of his sixth day in the saddle, Remme exchanged a tired horse for a fresh one at French Prairie. Established by retired

French Canadian trappers of the Hudson Bay Company, the settlement was populated by men and women who knew the cattle trader by sight. He answered greetings from several men while he wolfed down a quick breakfast and by noon he was in Milwaukie, Oregon after leaving Willamette Falls in Oregon City behind.

There on the banks of the Willamette River Remme could see that the river was high, swollen and angry with spring flood waters. Anchored next to a wooden landing was the log ferry that transported men, cattle and supplies across the river. It was a floating contraption constructed of big, heavy fir logs, fully five feet thick, locked together by iron spikes four feet long. The spikes were driven through the wooden planking deep into the logs which were reinforced with thick rope bindings. Side rails six feet high formed barriers on both sides of the raft to keep barnyard animals and horses from falling into the water. Power to move the ferry back and forth across the river came from a system of ropes and pulleys that reached from one side of the Willamette to the other. By pulling on the ropes in one direction, the ferryman launched the raft from the east side of the river to the west bank. When he embarked from Portland to cross back to

Milwaukie, he hauled in the opposite direction. The thick ropes also served another purpose: they prevented the raft from drifting too far off of its course.

A man who Remme assumed was the operator of the ferry stepped out of a small shack that was built on the wooden landing. A spare, long-legged individual with a dour expression, he looked up at Remme and said, "If you're thinking about getting across, forget it. Ain't no amount of money could make me try that river high as it is."

Remme was stunned. So close and yet so far! He eased his horse closer to the ferry landing and said earnestly, "Mister, I've ridden more than 700 miles to cross this river to get to Portland. I can't wait for the river to go down. I've got to get to Portland now."

The ferryman frowned. "What's so important that it can't wait a day or so?"

"Everything I own depends on it," Remme said desperately. "If you won't take me across I'll have to swim across with my horse." The quality of conviction in Remme's voice made the ferryman look up into his eyes. Startled, he peered more closely at Remme, taking in the cattle trader's mud-smeared clothes, the horse lather stains spreading from his belt buckle to his knees and the anxiety in his frank, black eyes. The ferryman turned to look at the strong, swift, muddy water rushing by. The current carried limbs of trees, splintered logs and tufts of grass. Small leaves bobbed and fluttered like green flags on the choppy surface.

He heaved a sigh and said to Remme, "Get your horse on board. You'll have to help with the ropes. If we get hit by a big log or the strain's too much for the ropes and she tears loose, you'll have to pay for the damage, that is—if we don't drown."

Remme nodded; he couldn't speak. The last hurdle had fallen. He dismounted and led his horse, clattering nervously, onto the ferry and tied the reins to a bar in one of the side rails. He stood behind the ferryman, and like him, took a firm grasp on the ropes and pulled. He was surprised at how easy it was to get the barge moving. He felt the power of the river a minute later when the two of them had hauled the ferry out of its calm shelter by the landing. The barge shuddered and creaked loudly when the river grabbed it. The strength of both men was required to keep the ropes moving; Remme could see them smacking the water in front of the ferry and soon his arms and shirt were dripping with water that ran off the wet ropes as they passed through his hands after being pulled by the ferryman.

It was when they were in midstream, navigating through a tricky and dangerous section of fast water that Remme heard a sound that brought a cry of despair from his lips.

Boom! Boom!

"Is that the *Columbia?*" he yelled, beseeching the ferryman for an answer.

"Don't stop pulling!" the man shouted. "Keep a steady strain. It could be the *Columbia.* Sometimes they fire the canon when she's just been sighted. Other times when she's docked. Can't tell till you get there."

Bending his back over the whip-cracking ropes and peering anxiously through the wet wind spray off the river, Remme could not see the shape of the steamer. Where was it? He could spot a few buildings, but the docks where the big boats tied up were upstream from the place the ferry landed.

A few minutes later the ponderous barge entered calmer water and the ferryman said, "I'll take her in by myself."

Remme dropped his arms amazed at the ache in his muscles. Work he was not used to seemed a lark for the ferryman. When the ferryman asked Remme for the crossing fee of two dollars, one for Remme's horse and one for Remme, the Frenchman placed a $10 gold piece in the man's outstretched hand.

The ferryman looked at the coin and then at Remme who was climbing aboard his horse. "I didn't do it for the money," he said.

"I know that and I'm grateful," Remme answered. Then he waved his hand in a salute and kneed his pony into a run. Fifteen minutes after leaving the ferry behind, Remme handed the reins of his horse to the liveryman at Stewart's Stable. He was almost afraid to ask the question he had put to the ferryman. "The *Columbia* — has she arrived?"

"She's just been sighted," the man said casually. "You can always tell, they fire a canon."

Remme got directions to the Adams Express office and started running down the street before the stablehand's last words were out of his mouth.

He stopped to calm himself and collect his wits as he saw the sign above the door with the painted letters: Adams Express Company. Squaring his shoulders and taking a deep breath, he reached for the door knob.

Oh God, he shuddered as the knob refused to turn in his hand. Locked! The door was locked! Cold fear, utter despair gripped him. Was it possible that the news of the failure of Adams Express had reached Portland by some other means than the *Columbia?* It seemed impossible, and yet? What other explanation could there be for the disaster that confronted him? He swallowed hard and actually felt chilled, faint. For a moment he couldn't catch his breath. To lose at the very last moment was unfair. It was wrong. It was almost more than he could bear. Suddenly angry, he reached for the knob to rattle the door when he heard a voice behind him. Remme whirled and saw a man wearing glasses and dressed in a dark brown suit and a small-brimmed grey hat.

"Hello, may I help you?" he asked. "I'm Dr. Steinberger. I've been to lunch."

By shear will power, Remme forced his voice to sound casual. How many hours had he dreamed of this moment while he swayed in the saddle listening to the creak of leather beneath him?

"I'd like to get a draft cashed. I've bought a herd of cattle and the longer I wait to pay for them the worse off I am."

"Come in."

Remme followed numbly thinking of the minutes ticking by as the *Columbia* edged up the river to dock. Was she alongside now, deck hands lowering the gangplank for the passengers to disembark? His throat was dry as he extracted his certificate of deposit from its hiding place in the oilskin packet next to his chest.

The agent took Remme's draft and examined it leisurely from behind his money counter. He cocked an eye at Remme who certainly looked authentic, mud spattered, smelling strongly of horse lather, and tough-looking for his short wiry height. Then Steinberger held the draft up to the light and peered at it intently. Finally turning it face up, he noted the signature of W. B. Rochester, the Adams agent in Sacramento.

"Looks authentic," he said. "Let's see," he added, figuring on a pad with a pencil. "That's $12,500 less my agents commission of one half percent. That comes to $62.50. That'll be $12,437.50 net to you." The agent pushed the pad across the counter. "See if you agree with those figures," he said.

Remme stared at the pad numbly and merely nodded. Surely by now the *Columbia* had docked. The purser was probably on a dead run from the boat right this minute with the news of the bankruptcy.

"Hurry, man, hurry!" he screamed at the agent

in his mind.

From his safe Dr. Steinberger unhurriedly trans-ferred several stacks of gold to the counter top, then trimmed them evenly with his fingers so that each pile of gold slugs stood in a small, neat twinkling column. He stepped back slightly, pleased with the commission he had earned.

Remme could not control the violent trembling of his hands as he scooped up the piles of $50 gold slugs. For even as they fell into his saddle bags, he heard the pounding of running foot steps, and as he slung the heavy leather bags over his shoulder and stepped outside, he saw Ralph Meade, purser of the *Columbia,* red-faced and breathless, waving a piece of paper. He brushed past Remme to confront Dr. Steinberger, but it was too late. Louis Remme had won an impossible race of almost 700 miles—by a margin of less than three minutes.

The depositors of Adams Express Company in Oregon never received any money after the single payment to Remme on February 29, 1855. As for him, he went on to prosper as a cattle trader and his remarkable ride became one of the legends of the American West. Descendants of old Oregon pio-neers like to tell about Louis Remme on long winter nights beside roaring oak fires when the smoke and dancing flames seem to call up pictures of a lonely man on a fast horse riding like the wind to save his gold.